TOKYO HEARTS

Renae Lucas-Hall is an Australian born British novelist and writer. After graduating from university with a degree in Japanese Language and Culture, she lived in Tokyo for two years and taught English. Over the past twenty years, Renae has continued to visit Japan many times for work or as a tourist. She lives in Gloucestershire in the UK with her husband and their Siberian Husky.

For more about Renae and her next novel, please go to www.renaelucashall.com

TOKYO HEARTS

by

Renae Lucas-Hall

**Grosvenor House
Publishing Limited**

This book is published by
Grosvenor House Publishing Ltd
28-30 High Street, Guildford, Surrey, GU1 3EL.
www.grosvenorhousepublishing.co.uk

A CIP record for this book
is available from the British Library

ISBN 978-1-78148-769-3

....

Cover artwork by Cathy Helms www.avalongraphics.org
Cover image by Svetlana Turilova, copyright Deposit Photos

....

The proverbs in this book were extracted from:

Yamamoto T, (2007) Nichiei Hikaku Kotowaza Jishin (Japanese-English Comparison Proverb Cyclopedia). Ōsaka, Japan: Sogensha Publishing.

....

....

CHAPTER 1

That which comes from the heart will go to the heart

On the last tempestuous Thursday in July, Takashi discovered the difference between the type of girl that a boy could like and the type of woman that a man could love.

The whole of Tokyo was heaving from the combination of heavy rain and sweltering humidity. Takashi climbed the slippery stairs to the café where he would soon meet up with Haruka and hoped that the summer rainy season would end this week. His light, waterproof jacket had helped him brave the elements that day, but his jeans were now soaked and clinging uncomfortably to his legs. His wet hair was dripping down the back of his neck.

Takashi was a good-looking young man. He had big eyes, the colour of dark chocolate. His hair was dead straight, very short and as black as ink. The bridge of his nose was a bit flat and his nostrils were small. His skin was clear, yet there was a slight puffiness around his eyes that spoke of long hours studying in a smoky and cramped apartment. Takashi was particularly proud of his mid-ear sideburns, which added balance to his face. Not many Japanese men could boast of having sideburns as thick as his. He always made sure they were the right shape and length after every shave. Takashi was also kind and honest and considered himself to be a proper gentleman. He'd learned from watching the occasional American black-and-white movie, featuring Gene Kelly or Fred Astaire, how to open the door for a lady, pull out her chair at a table and even how to expertly use a knife and fork.

Takashi shook himself dry at the entrance inside the café. After sitting down on the closest lounge next to the door, he flicked out a Mild Seven cigarette, cocking his head as he lit it. Inhaling and exhaling deeply on every puff, he thought about the phone call he'd had with Haruka's father on Monday. He'd told Takashi that Haruka was out having lunch with her ex-boyfriend from Kyoto. She'd mentioned to him in past conversations that she had a friend in Kyoto, but Takashi clearly remembered her saying that he was only a friend.

Thinking about this ex-boyfriend made Takashi nervous as he waited for Haruka to arrive. It bothered him that she'd never referred to her friend in Kyoto as an ex-boyfriend in the past. He'd met Haruka at university and the combination of her good looks and sincerity had really impressed Takashi from the start. There'd never been any secrets between them.

She'd had plenty of opportunities to mention this ex-boyfriend to him years ago in their lectures, where they'd often whispered behind cupped hands, not wanting to attract the lecturer's attention, as they'd shared their likes and dislikes, their dreams and disappointments. He thought to himself that she'd had more than enough time to say something about him at the university cafeteria where they'd spent hour upon hour discussing their past, present and future. She'd also had the opportunity to talk about him during many of their phone calls over the years.

From the moment Takashi had first met Haruka, she'd always been straight with him. She'd never come across as a person who would mislead others. At university, if someone was friendly towards her, only because they'd wanted to borrow her lecture notes, she'd never got too close to them. During team-building exercises, Haruka would always complete more than her share of work. She'd arrive early to meet up with the group, full of ideas, holding reams of paper typed up with the expected composition for their reports, ready to assist any others who couldn't cope and even help complete her friends' assignments if they couldn't deal with the workload. Other team members would phone at the last minute with a variety of poor but well-rehearsed excuses, but this had never been Haruka's style. Yes, she'd always been honest with Takashi and everyone that they'd known, so Takashi had to ask himself again: why had she never mentioned this ex-boyfriend?

Haruka would soon be by his side and Takashi was keen to have a conversation with her about past boyfriends. They'd arranged to meet every Thursday at six thirty p.m. in this same café in Omotesando for the last three weeks. A month ago, Takashi had spent an hour walking through Harajuku and Omotesando, looking for the perfect place to meet up with her. He hadn't wanted to meet her somewhere that was too busy or too quiet. He'd finally decided on a café close to Omotesando's subway exit. It was easy to find above the clothing boutiques Sisley and Morgan de Toi. He thought that it was important to find a café in this area because Haruka adored shopping and like most young Japanese girls, clearly loved her brands.

Takashi was quite pleased with himself for finding this chic meeting spot. Café hors et dans was its name. He'd learnt from Haruka the week before that this was French for "Inside and Out Coffee Shop". At the top of the stairs was an open-air area paved in stone, with eleven tables and two benches set out to welcome customers on warm and sultry evenings. On those drier nights, his favourite place to sit was at one of the counters outside on the balcony overlooking the street below. From there, he could look out and see Haruka approach from the train station or step out from one of the shops nearby. Most of the famous boutiques had transparent front windows and on clearer days, Takashi could clearly see inside them. Fendi, Celine, Gucci, Hanae Mori, Shu Uemura and Emporio Armani were some of the international brands displayed along this famous shopping strip.

Four weeks ago, when he'd first entered this café, he'd instantly known that Haruka would like it. The interior was stylish, the customers were all well-dressed and very sophisticated and the staff seemed attentive yet not intrusive. It interested him that this café was most often filled almost entirely with young fashionistas. There were usually two types of trends here, both blending in well with each other; each respecting the other for their individual style. Those that came from Omotesando, dressed in the subtle shades of Yohji Yamamoto and Comme des Garçons. The other set, those who wore individual pieces that they had picked up in the markets of Harajuku – their clothes were brash, their jewellery outlandish and no one could help but look at them. It was not only their appearance that screamed *look at me*; it was the confidence in their voices and their shrill shrieks that said that they believed they were the future.

A waiter in long black trousers, a white shirt and black vest with thick, 1960s-style black glasses approached Takashi. 'What would you like to drink?' He asked.

'An iced coffee with an extra sugar syrup please,' Takashi replied.

'Would you like anything to eat?'

'No thank you.'

Takashi stubbed out his cigarette and, noticing a magazine stand near the bar, he picked out a book on stylish hotels in Paris by Herbert Ypma. He could see others on another stand near the door on Barcelona and Provence in France. Takashi knew Haruka liked everything European, so if there were ever a time when either of them was waiting for the other, he thought that they could browse through some interesting books without looking conspicuously alone. He didn't like to admit it, but he was a little nervous that day, so this book that he was reading now, although beautiful to look at, didn't really hold his attention.

Takashi looked up and around the room, darting his eyes about, not wanting to stare at the other customers, as he tapped the table in anticipation. This evening, a balding man in an expensive pinstripe suit sat in front of him, chatting up a young girl in a mini-skirt who looked only seventeen or eighteen years old. To their left were two slick businesswomen – one in a black silk suit; the other in a flowing white jacket and a tulip-shaped skirt. Up on the landing, under cover, was a crowd of five young men drinking beer, all of them in skinny jeans and multi-coloured shirts. One of the five had a shaved pattern imprinted on the right side of his head. To their right, two young businessmen in well-cut navy suits were exchanging business cards.

Behind the bar, the waiter with the thick black glasses stood casually yet attentively, preparing his coffee with a waitress who kept shooting him looks. Takashi stared straight at her and their eyes met for a moment. She blushed and looked away. The waitress quickly went back to polishing glasses and he went back to looking around the room, trying not to look like he was staring at anyone in particular.

The waiter came over and placed Takashi's coffee, some extra sugar syrups and a glass of iced water in front of him. Takashi thanked him and the waiter honoured him with a short bow before returning to his position behind the bar. Takashi poured the liquid sugar into his cold drink and slowly stirred it as he continued to look around the café. He noticed that there were woven baskets under each of the seats for coats and bags, something that he hadn't seen before. The ceiling had an industrial design with exposed air-conditioning tubes painted white. Eclectic gift boxes were sitting on top of exposed walls of stone. Underneath, screen prints of leaves in indigo and orange were strategically placed around this split-level café. A version of "The Girl from Ipanema" performed by Frank Sinatra and the maestro Antonio Carlos Jobim was playing in the background, and this music made him feel like he was not in Tokyo at all.

It was still only six twenty p.m. Haruka would be arriving soon. She was always very punctual. Takashi liked to arrive half an hour early, not only to watch the ever-changing cast of characters that came together here, but also to watch Haruka come through the door and see her smile as she approached him.

Haruka Yoshino was one of the most sought-after girls at university. Takashi had met her in his first-year Marketing lecture. She'd only completed one year because her father had become so ill at the time, but she'd left such an impression on him that he'd stayed in touch with her. Even now, he wasn't sure if they were just friends or whether she considered these meetings as dates. He knew he certainly wanted to date her.

Takashi's mobile phone vibrated against his thigh. Thinking it might be a message from Haruka, he was quick to check for a call or a text. It wasn't from her. His mother had sent him a reminder telling him to come out to Yokosuka on Saturday to spend some time with his grandmother. This would mean an uncomfortably long train journey in stifling humidity and several hours spent with his one and only remaining grandparent from his father's side, who'd always chastised him and who had often complained about his upbringing.

The time on his mobile phone showed it was now 6:30 p.m.

Two minutes later, Haruka walked through the doors of the café with her usual dignified grace. She tied her umbrella with one swift movement and passed the waiters at the bar, coming towards him as if there was no one else in the room. Takashi watched her approach as he stood to greet her, appreciating the perfect neatness that she always represented. Her face glistened from the humidity outside and as she came closer, he marvelled at the way the raindrops on the end of her eyelashes gave her a certain glow. Miraculously, her clothes and the Yohji Yamamoto shopping bag she casually held onto were mostly dry, despite the heavy rain that was still constant outside. They were both twenty-one years old, yet Haruka held the mystique of someone more mature. At five feet, she was not quite as tall as Takashi. Her lissom figure and delicate features supported a swan-like neck. Her high cheekbones and light skin tone complemented her honey brown eyes that were offset by her long, flowing and lustrous black hair.

It suddenly occurred to Takashi that it was only because of Haruka's total lack of intimidation that she was so often able to pass through crowds unnoticed. Today, however, her anonymity was soon disclosed.

'Hi there, Takashi,' she said. 'I just....' Haruka tripped on the leg of the table, dropped her shopping bag and lost her balance as she bumped her knee against the table's corner. Her handbag also fell open onto the lounge and Takashi reached out to steady her. The waiter with the black 1960s-style glasses ran over to assist her, asking over and over again if she was all right. The couple at the table opposite, the young girl and the much older man, turned to watch her stumble for a moment before returning to their own private conversation.

'Are you okay now?' Takashi asked, concerned that she might have bruised her leg.

'Fine, thanks,' she replied with a self-conscious laugh. She rubbed her left shin. Haruka's purse and keys had fallen out. Takashi returned them to her and she put them back inside her handbag and zipped it safely shut.

Takashi looked at her beautiful face. Her eyes were sweetly expressive and her lips were rosy. She took off her white linen jacket and sat down, smoothing her cream skirt over and under her knees. It looked like she was going to say something and then she stopped herself. She said nothing. It was only the flush of her cheeks and the way her lips curled up slightly at each corner in parentheses that told Takashi how happy she was to see him again.

'Thanks for coming,' Takashi said to her. He was grateful that she was there. Every time they were meant to meet, he was always afraid she'd change her mind at the last minute and fail to show up. He often felt that she was just too good to be true, and somehow he didn't deserve her company.

'I always like meeting up with you,' said Haruka. 'You look well.'

'I had a shower and a shave before I came out. I wanted to look good for you ... by the way – are my sideburns straight?' Takashi asked her, turning his head from side to side for her to inspect them.

'They're perfect,' said Haruka. She leant forward and touched each side of his face softly with her left index finger and nodded her head approvingly.

'Great. I was worried they weren't the same length,' said Takashi, blushing deeply as he felt her stroke each side of his face. 'It's warm in here, don't you think?' he said to her, trying to find an excuse for the sudden rush of colour in his cheeks.

'Yes, you're right,' replied Haruka, whose face was also tinged in pink.

'You've been shopping?' Takashi asked her, nodding at the Yohji Yamamoto bag at her side.

'I bought a new skirt after work. I needed new clothes for the summer and I've had my eye on this for a couple of months.' She pulled the material out for Takashi to admire. 'Feel this material ... it's so soft ... and this navy colour is just right ... and look at the stitching.'

'How much was it? It looks expensive,' said Takashi.

'That's the beauty of it – it doesn't look cheap.'

'But you could buy a skirt in one of the small boutiques in Harajuku for half the price.'

'That's true but no one can create the asymmetric designs like Yamamoto, and look at the embroidery and the quality of the fabric. This will last me twenty years, and it will never go out of fashion.'

She was so convinced she'd made a good purchase that Takashi could not find the words to contradict her.

The waitress approached with an extra glass of iced water and Haruka ordered an iced tea. Her voice was soft and silky. When the tea arrived, she sat quietly and nodded as Takashi told her about his studies at university. He really wanted to discuss the ex-boyfriend her father had mentioned during his phone call with him on Monday. However, it did not seem to be the right time or place and he was afraid of upsetting a perfectly happy Thursday evening. Instead, he decided to continue sharing his feelings about his studies and his future. He knew she would be supportive.

'It won't be long before I finish university and I feel that so many unusual changes are happening,' said Takashi. 'I sometimes feel that instead of going forward, I feel like I'm going backwards in time.'

'What do you mean, Takashi?'

'Well, I've cut my long hair short again. I've stripped the blonde out of it and now I have a hairstyle just like I used to wear it in my junior high school days.'

'I like it either way,' said Haruka.

'Thanks, but I feel that my faded jeans and lumberjack boots look stupid with this conservative hairstyle. What makes it even worse is that my mother is delighted with the new look and she said that I look like my father, minus the grey!' They both threw their heads back at the same time and laughed together at his comment.

'It's not all bad, though, Haruka. I don't really care if I've started to resemble my father. I suppose it's time that I started growing up. I knew that I'd have to conform for the future. My mother says I need to consider my responsibilities.'

'You might start wearing a very conservative shirt and tie and then go out and buy a people carrier!' said Haruka. They laughed again as Takashi tried to imagine this.

Takashi lowered his voice and went on to tell Haruka that his only regret was that he already felt a slight distance between his high school friends and himself. Akira had been abroad for three years now; he was studying in America. Masaya had just opened a tavern in Shimokitazawa financed by his father, and Kenji was working full time at his family's restaurant in the exclusive Ginza district. All three of his friends had much more exciting lives, and they were doing exactly what they wanted to do whenever they wanted to do it.

'When I started at university, I had high hopes of doing really well and enjoying my course,' Takashi said. 'But

I didn't expect the Marketing exams to be so difficult. I try to prepare for them, but on the days I plan to do a lot of study, I realise by the evening that I've only completed a small part of what I'd hoped to get through.'

Takashi had never been a shy or reserved person, but in contrast to the spirited enthusiasm he shared with his high school friends, he now felt that the burden of his studies had taken away his hopes for a brighter future.

'I'm sure you'll be fine,' said Haruka. 'I remember you doing really well in first year at university. Do you remember the time you helped me prepare for a Logistics exam? You spent hours going through it in the university library with me and you grasped the concepts so much better than I did. I think you're being too hard on yourself.'

'Thanks, Haruka. What are your plans for the future?' Every girl Takashi had dated over the last couple of years either wanted to travel or start a course of study. Haruka was a modern girl. Surely she, too, had exciting plans for the next few years.

'I've decided that I want to settle down, get married and have children,' replied Haruka with such surety that it took him by surprise.

Marriage and children! Takashi was impressed – very impressed. This girl was not into playing games with him or anyone else. He looked into her eyes and saw a maturity and warmth. Up until now, he'd seen Haruka as a very pretty girl that he'd wanted to take out even show off to his friends, but now, looking into her eyes, he wondered whether he wanted more than that. There was a connection here that made him feel closer to her, and for the first time he felt completely at ease with a woman.

'Do you want to know what I dream about when I think about the future?' Haruka asked him.

'Definitely, tell me,' Takashi replied.

'Like a lot of girls, I have big dreams for my wedding day. I'd really like to get married in a Western-style Vera Wang wedding dress or maybe a gown by Eri Matsui – I went with a friend who was getting married to her studio in Aoyama and I was blown away by some of her designs. They're mathematically engineered, so the dresses have an ethereal, floating effect. I've put a lot of thought into this, Takashi, and I think I'd also like to wear a pure white silk shiro-maku wedding kimono for the ceremony. Afterwards, I'd put on a colourful and elaborate red uchikake for the wedding reception ... maybe embroidered with plum blossoms or cranes,' she said.

'I think you'd look beautiful in a kimono,' Takashi told her.

'On top of this, I'd like the long silk obi sash to be made from intricate brocade,' she continued, 'and it would be so fine that it would cost at least twice as much as the kimono.'

'Very expensive, but I'm sure that would be very nice ... and where would you like to live?' Takashi asked.

'As you know, I've grown up in Ōfune so I'm not sure if I'd like to live right in the centre of Tokyo, but I would like a house in a good area where I could easily get into Tokyo.'

'I completely understand that, having grown up in Yokosuka.'

'And I'd like to live in a two-storey detached house with a pretty Japanese garden – I don't mind if the garden is small,' continued Haruka.

'A garage would be good, too – somewhere to park the car,' said Takashi.

'Yes, and there would be a tall, thick hedge around the garden to protect our privacy, and the house would have all the conveniences of a Western house, but it would also have some Japanese features. There would be Western-style furniture in some of the rooms, but there would also be two or three tatami rooms, and in the bathroom, there would be a Japanese ofuro bath.'

Takashi's heart was beating loudly in his chest. He was sure Haruka had just said the garden hedge in her dream house needed to protect *their* privacy. Maybe she could see him in her future, just as he could see her in his.

'Haruka, how about you and I....'

Haruka interrupted. 'Did you feel that? It felt like an earthquake.' She held onto the edge of the table with one hand and grabbed Takashi's hand with the other.

'Yes, you're right,' said Takashi. The floor beneath them had definitely shuddered. He'd wanted to talk about their friendship moving on to the next level, but he was just as happy to be holding Haruka's hand, if only for a couple of minutes. Her fingers felt soft and fragile. Her gentle clutch made him feel like her protector. The room vibrated once again, but not enough to scare Takashi. He looked at Haruka's concerned face and smiled at her with reassurance. Everyone in the café was tense, and the room fell silent for a minute as they all waited to see what might happen next. The rumbling soon dissipated and Haruka took back her hand. Takashi would have liked to hold onto her hand for the rest of the evening.

'I'll be back in a moment,' Haruka said, nodding towards the ladies' room.

'Okay,' Takashi said softly. 'But come straight back if you feel any more tremors.'

The waiter came over to fill up their glasses of water and as he did so, Takashi noticed a white envelope on the floor by his feet. **Junko – Shibuya** was written across it. It was open and he picked it up and counted five ¥10,000 notes inside. It must have belonged to Haruka and fallen out of her bag when she tripped.

Five minutes later, Haruka came back to the table. Takashi looked up to see her, her mouth open with disbelief, staring at the envelope that he was waving in the air from the lounge where he was waiting for her.

'Does this belong to you?' Takashi asked her with a grin.

'Yes, it's really important,' she replied. 'I have to take it to Shibuya in the morning before work. Where'd you find it?'

'I just picked it up off the floor. It must have fallen out of your bag when you tripped.'

'You're the best, Takashi, thanks so much,' she said to him.

Anyone loves flattery, but because it came from Haruka, he was delighted.

'It looks like there won't be any major earthquakes tonight. Are you okay now?' he asked her.

'I'm fine, thanks,' she replied.

Takashi still wanted to talk to her further about matters of the heart. He really wanted her to fill in the details about the ex-boyfriend and also find out about how she felt about him.

'Tell me, what are you doing on the weekend?' he asked, hoping she might shine a light on this mystery man from Kyoto and if she was planning to go out with him. 'Are you spending time with anyone interesting?'

'My mother and I have our Ikebana flower arrangement class on Saturday. What about you, Takashi? What are your plans for the weekend?'

It was going to be more difficult than he thought trying to find out about this guy from Kyoto. He'd have to be more direct, but in doing so, he'd have to gently steer the conversation away from his life in order to find out more about her plans.

'I have to go out to Yokosuka and visit my grandmother,' said Takashi, realising as he said this that it would be difficult to change the flow of conversation from grandmothers to her love interests.

'Didn't you once tell me that your grandmother in Yokosuka is your only surviving grandparent?'

'Yes, you have a good memory, Haruka. I guess I feel a sense of duty towards her. I never enjoy visiting her, but I feel I'm forced to by my parents. Last time I went to see her, she looked so fragile and I felt sorry for her, but it's always so difficult to please her. Even though my mother and I bend over backwards to try and make her happy, we can never do anything right in her eyes. She's not all bad though, she does dote on my father, so she is capable of kindness. Anyway, that's my plans for the weekend. It will be pretty boring.'

'I understand, Takashi. Neither of us has brothers nor sisters, so I suppose the duties fall more heavily on us where family is concerned.'

'It's difficult growing up without a brother or sister,' Takashi continued. He'd never told Haruka about his brother, who'd passed away when he was a lot younger. 'One day I'd like to have at least two children with the right woman – someone who is kind and caring.' He placed his hand over hers. 'Haruka, you're so special,' he started to say. 'I hope that you feel the same way about me.'

Haruka looked surprised and pulled gently away from him, and he regretted having said those words. 'I like you too, Takashi, but....'

Haruka hesitated, so Takashi couldn't help finishing her sentence. 'There's someone else?' He started to ask, with a quiet hope that she would correct him, but she didn't.

Oh no, Takashi thought to himself. He'd been too direct and now he'd embarrassed her. He thought that he should really change the subject. But he couldn't help himself and he continued to push Haruka for a more definitive answer. 'So ... there's no one else, is there?' he asked her, realising how pathetic he must have sounded and wishing that he'd never said anything.

Haruka's face went bright red. Takashi scratched his left ear furiously. She shifted in her seat uncomfortably. He wondered why she didn't reassure him.

Instead, she awkwardly changed the direction of this conversation with a statement that surprised him.

'I think you'd like to go out with me because you pity me,' she said to him abruptly.

'Of course not, why would I pity you?' he put to her with some indignation.

'Because I had to look after my father and I couldn't continue at university,' she said, with sadness and also with humiliation.

Takashi was confused, but he thought that this was a good time to tell Haruka about his brother. He had to explain this because he certainly didn't want her to think that he felt this way about her because of pity.

'I don't pity you at all,' Takashi tried to assure her. 'I understand what you went through because I had a similar situation with my older brother.'

'An older brother!' she exclaimed. 'I've never heard you speak about him. I thought that you were an only child.' Haruka leaned forward and showed Takashi that she was listening intently.

Maybe it wouldn't be so difficult for him to explain to her about what had happened to his brother Yasuo, Takashi thought to himself.

'I had an older brother, but he passed away. He would have been twenty-six this year if he was still with us. He was sick for quite a long time. He had Hodgkin's disease,' he told her.

'Oh, I'm so sorry, Takashi,' she replied. 'I didn't know.'

'It's okay. I just know that it's difficult to look after a sick family member. Yasuo – that was his name – went through a lot before he died. He lost a lot of weight, his lymph nodes were enlarged, his whole body was itchy all the time and then he went through radiation therapy and chemotherapy. At one point, we thought he was going to recover, but the disease claimed him and he passed away when he was fifteen. I didn't understand a lot at the time. I was only ten, but it was difficult.'

Haruka looked at him with compassion. He knew that she would understand. 'Thanks for telling me this. It's obviously difficult for you to talk about,' she said.

Haruka's beautiful eyes that looked at him now so kindly somehow helped him feel better about his brother.

'I have some news to share with you, Takashi. The English conversation school that I work for has a management position available and they think that I should apply. It would mean I would have a lot more responsibilities, which I've always wanted, and my salary would be considerably better. There's a catch though, Takashi. The job is in Kyoto,' Haruka said to him. She watched his face lose its happy expression and the colour in his cheeks disappear.

'You must be really excited,' Takashi said quietly, looking down at his shoes. He tried to balance his feelings of upset with how he knew she needed him to share in her excitement. He tried to force out a smile, but Haruka caught his disappointment and placed her hand on his knee.

'I know you work really hard and you love your job, so you deserve it,' Takashi said to her without a lot of enthusiasm. He really wanted to tell her not to take the job, but he knew it would be difficult to convince her to stay in Tokyo if this was something she really wanted. 'Isn't there a management position in Tokyo that you could take? Your company has branches in every major town here.'

'I'm afraid not,' said Haruka.

'Well, when would you have to start if you took the job in Kyoto? Is it a permanent position?' he asked.

'I'm not sure when they'd like me to start or whether it would be permanent. My manager talked with me a couple of days ago about the job and I know that she went to quite a lot of trouble to get me an interview with the manager in Kyoto. She has given me a couple of weeks to think about it and talk it over with my family, as she knows I still live at home.'

Takashi was lost for words. Just when they'd started to meet up again and he could see their relationship advancing to the next stage; it looked like he was going to lose his chance of getting closer to his dream woman. He looked at his watch and realised that they'd been sitting there for over ninety minutes. It was funny how the time always flew by when he was with Haruka.

It was just after eight p.m. and Takashi started to feel a chill, sitting in this air-conditioned café. He looked around and the faces had changed around him; the younger groups that had surrounded him an hour before had been replaced by an older, more sophisticated set. Knowing that Haruka had a long journey ahead of her on the Yokosuka line back to Ōfune, he suggested that they should head home. He helped her into her jacket and they headed out into the street.

The rain had stopped and the air did not feel as heavy and dense now. Takashi suggested that they walk past the shops to Harajuku station. He walked as closely as he could to Haruka without their hands touching. It felt like he was moving in slow motion. Whether it was the weather or being with Haruka, he wasn't quite sure. It just felt like he was walking in a trance. He would have liked to hold her hand, but she was clutching her handbag on her right shoulder and carrying the Yohji Yamamoto shopping bag on her left wrist. It would have looked awkward and unnatural for him to even try and reach out to her.

Every time a breeze lifted, Takashi inhaled deeply, but not noticeably, trying to catch the floral scent of Haruka's perfume. He wanted to remember that sweet smell of jasmine over the next few days until they would meet again the following week.

They reached Harajuku train station. Haruka had a train pass, but waited as Takashi bought a ticket from the machine. He turned and thanked her for meeting him and told her he was already looking forward to the following week and she gave him the sweetest smile. Haruka turned and disappeared through the barrier into the crowd of commuters looking for her platform.

Often it is quite obvious to others when you're in love. Your complexion is clearer and your face lights up. A lot of people looked at Takashi as he stood watching Haruka leave that day. A lot of people looked at him and smiled.

But it wasn't long before Takashi's dreamlike state went to pieces after he boarded his train. Reality set in and he realised Haruka had never answered his question properly when he'd asked her if there was someone else she was interested in. Not knowing the answer to this hurt, and he didn't like the feelings of jealousy welling up inside of him. On top of this, the news of Haruka applying for a job in Kyoto meant he was moving backwards instead of forwards, and all his plans for the dream life that he'd envisioned were no longer a foreseeable reality. He vowed to himself that he would make every effort the following Thursday to rectify the situation and show Haruka how much he cared about her.

CHAPTER 2

He carries two faces under one hood

Haruka changed trains at Shinagawa and took the Yokosuka line for Ōfune. She was pleased to find a seat next to the door after stepping into the carriage. A much older lady with a lined face, hinting of a long life full of a thousand stories, sat down next to her. Haruka had a lengthy journey ahead of her – it was at least an hour before she would arrive at her stop. She sat with her knees touching and her heels together and smoothed out her skirt, resting her handbag on her lap. Six years of ballet lessons until the age of twelve had taught her good posture. She was proud of the fact that she'd trained her body to sit, stand, walk and lie in positions that would ensure she'd never suffer from back pain.

Haruka sighed. She was tired but content. It had been a lovely evening. She shut her eyes, wanting to avoid the scene in front of her. The heavy humidity of the day had taken its toll on the surrounding passengers, and the air was thick and stifling.

Tightening the clutch on her handbag and shuffling a little in her seat in order not to appear asleep, she thought about her time with Takashi. In her mind, she saw his kind face – his strong jaw set below his firm mouth. She smiled as she pictured his gentle dark brown eyes and small, flat nose. His square shoulders against his lean, sinewy body. Haruka liked the way his cheeks flushed when he felt uncomfortable and the way he would scratch his left ear when he was nervous. She also thought his bushy sideburns were very sexy. Every time Haruka met up with Takashi, she enjoyed his company. They certainly had a lot in common. They were both interested in studying Marketing. They shared a love of all things Japanese, whether it was cultural, historical, religious or otherwise. They both came from loving families and had similar aspirations for the future. They both loved the idea of travelling and learning about other cultures and Takashi lacked the selfishness and arrogance of so many other boys his age.

Haruka really thought of herself as very lucky to have a friend like Takashi. They'd met for the first time at the beginning of term in her first and only year at university. He could have chosen to sit next to any number of girls, yet he'd taken a seat beside Haruka on the first day. From then on, they'd become great friends. The fact that their relationship was purely platonic helped create within her a respect for him that she did not know could exist until recently.

Takashi had been and always would be a great friend for Haruka, a soothing constant in her life. Able to read between the lines, he'd always been there to support her when she needed him most. She'd realised this two years ago when her father had a heart attack. He'd needed a total commitment from both her mother and herself to nurse him back to good health over a period of eighteen months.

Every week, Haruka would receive a call from Takashi. Her family were just starting to reach the point of despair over her father's condition, when one day, after speaking to Takashi, she found herself softly singing a tune when she walked into the room where her father was lying. As she set his lunch tray down next to his bed, her father smiled and managed with her help to sit up. Every day after that, she would sing a tune as she fussed over her father and made his room more comfortable, and every day her father got a little bit better.

Without Takashi's weekly calls, Haruka wouldn't have had the energy within her to get through those days or even carry one note of a song.

In the last couple of years, she'd been out with a series of boys, but most often for just one or two dates. She'd definitely had fun at the time. Yet looking back, she believed that she'd just been deceived into thinking she was special. Some boys would take her out, but only to impress their friends; others would flirt outrageously with her but did not ask her out – maybe having heard fallacious gossip spread by simple minds.

Takashi was very different. He was always kind and wanted to spend time with her for all the right reasons. She'd wanted to take their relationship further, but when the opportunity presented itself, she'd always recoiled at the thought that she might lose a close friend. She couldn't risk jeopardising the only relationship that had ever meant something significant to her. Thus, over the last few years Haruka hadn't dated anyone seriously.

Her life was much better now that her father had recovered from his illness and because of this she could now spend more time with friends whose company she enjoyed. But Haruka's life was about to become very complicated.

Haruka's ex-boyfriend Jun had come back into her life and she'd been out with him without Takashi's knowledge on several occasions. She'd met Jun when she was eighteen and they'd dated for a while. Her parents thought they were very well-suited at the time and before long there had been talk of an engagement. Haruka and her parents had even travelled to Kyoto to meet Jun's parents, but it was there that everything ended up turning out pear-shaped. When they'd returned to Tokyo, she had been very upset to hear that Jun's mother thought she was too young and immature for a serious commitment, and that had been the end of the relationship.

Thinking back to her first and last meeting with Jun's mother, Mrs Kurokawa, made her cheeks burn with shame even now. She could almost taste in her mouth the saltiness of the tears she'd shed on the day she'd ruined any chance of a commitment with Jun. It was all down to the fact that she'd sprained her ankle as she'd entered one of the finest restaurants in Kyoto, often frequented by Jun's family. Before the lunch, she'd spent the morning trying to be everything Jun's mother would want her to be, but as she and her parents walked through the entrance, ready to share their first meal with their future in-laws, Haruka's three-inch high heels had betrayed her and she'd lost her footing and sprained her ankle.

The pain in her left foot had been excruciating, and she'd cried out as the tears streamed down her cheeks. She could clearly remember peering up at Mrs Kurokawa, noticing her eyes shocked with humiliation, whilst she crouched down, holding her ankle in agony. Mrs Kurokawa had ordered her to pull herself together, and Haruka had really tried to suppress her suffering throughout the meal that followed, but she could not appreciate the food or the conversation as the stress on her left foot had killed her appetite entirely and her ability to communicate without wincing.

From that moment onwards, Mrs Kurokawa could only find fault in her. The morning she'd spent ingratiating herself with Jun's mother could not make up for her behaviour at the restaurant. Later that day, after the meal, Jun and her parents had taken her to the closest hospital in Kyoto because her ankle had swelled up to the point where it resembled a bruised mango. The doctor there, upon examination, had said that it was a serious sprain. Jun had been very sympathetic, and he'd tried to defend her, but he told her later that his mother wouldn't listen to him. Apparently, she couldn't forget her embarrassment when Haruka had made a scene at her favourite restaurant, where she was proud of the fact that all the waiters knew her name.

Jun and his mother were very close. He was her only child, and they had a real bond. His mother had spoiled him from an early age, and still continued to indulge him as an adult. He looked for her approval in all aspects of his life, whether it was the clothes he wore, the friends with whom he chose to be acquainted or the girls he dated. He really liked Haruka, but he was afraid of upsetting his mother, and so he was forced to quit seeing her.

Haruka truly liked Takashi, and she didn't want to hurt his feelings, but her parents had always been impressed by Jun and his family's wealth and they were encouraging her to spend more time with him. His full name was Junichiro Kurokawa, and she was flattered that he was visiting her again. Three years ago, after the breakup, she'd been devastated to lose him, but after a year of wondering how it all went wrong, she'd looked back at the time they'd spent together and she'd decided that they'd both been quite immature. She'd also thought that Jun was very critical of her and he'd teased her a lot. Haruka thought that he'd been trying to mould her into his version of what he'd like to have in a wife, rather than accepting her for who she really was. Now that they were seeing each other again, she believed that he'd changed for the better, and she was certainly a lot more mature.

Jun had started calling Haruka and visiting her again at her home in Ōfune for about two months now, and she couldn't say that she didn't enjoy the attention. She also knew that he made her mother happy. She liked Jun so much and always welcomed him into their house with open arms. The criticism that Haruka had received from Jun several years ago that had once annoyed her was now replaced with charm and compliments, and the generous presents that he brought with him from Kyoto on his visits were always a delight for her and her mother.

It was really difficult for Haruka to tell Takashi about her relationship with Jun. She could hardly tell him that he was poor and Jun was rich and this was an important factor when one was considering the ideal man to marry. Firstly, she didn't want to hurt his feelings, and secondly she didn't want anything to have a negative effect on their blossoming friendship.

Despite her best efforts, she knew Takashi was going to find out about Jun's interest in her sooner or later. Jun was always calling her on her mobile phone or dropping in unannounced at their house every time he stayed next door with his cousin, her neighbour and best friend Yuriko Makimoto.

Haruka could see why her mother would dote on Jun. She'd never really given up on the possibility of him as a future son-in-law. For starters, she knew he was very wealthy and generous. He also lived in an enviable and very spacious house in Kyoto that Haruka and her parents had marvelled at from the outside when they'd visited him and his parents. More recently, her mother was even more convinced of his wealth because he'd showed up at their house on several occasions bearing expensive gifts for her and her mother. Three weeks ago, he'd arrived at their house with presents from Tiffany & Co. Her mother was thrilled because, apart from the silver heart necklace he'd presented to Haruka, she'd received the same pendant in solid gold.

She opened her eyes and took a deep sigh. Reaching into her bag, she took out her English conversation textbook and began studying it on her lap. She was getting used to the various accents of some of the foreign teachers that worked at the English conversation school where she'd recently become employed, but she would have to improve her language skills if she wanted to take on extra responsibilities.

Haruka continued to have difficulty concentrating on her textbook on this crowded train. She realised that she was now sitting next to a very well-dressed businessman with an expensive gold watch. She couldn't help sneaking a better look at him. He had a large mole, the size of a hundred yen piece, on his left cheek, a double chin that draped over his tight collar, and he was sweating profusely under his fine gabardine jacket. He noticed Haruka glancing in his direction and gave her a slight nudge, while at the same time pointing at her English book.

'Are you learning English?' he asked her.

Haruka could smell his breath – it was putrid, and glancing to her right again, she saw large rings of sweat circling his armpits.

'Yes,' Haruka replied, wishing he hadn't asked her a question. She looked in the opposite direction towards the door.

'I could teach you to speak fluently. I lived in America for ten years,' he said – then added in English, in a thick accent, '*I am very good teacher.*'

'That's nice,' Haruka replied, a little sarcastically.

There was a line of people standing in front of her. She wanted to get up and escape, but the train was so crowded there was nowhere to go.

'Have you been overseas?' the sweaty man asked her.

'No,' replied Haruka.

'I could teach you English on the weekends. I won't even charge you. We could meet in a coffee shop. Where do you live?'

'I don't live near Tokyo,' Haruka lied, avoiding the question and hoping that he would now keep quiet.

'Do you come to Tokyo often?' he asked.

'No,' she replied, lying again.

A middle-aged woman standing in front of Haruka looked down with an amused expression.

'I live in Yokohama,' he said. He took out a business card from his shirt pocket and placed it on Haruka's book. 'Call me and we can be friends,' he said smiling nervously. Beads of sweat were sliding down the side of his face.

'If you live in Yokohama, you've just missed your stop,' Haruka pointed out to him. The train had just pulled out of Yokohama station.

'Yes, you're right. I ... um ... deliberately missed my stop because you're so beautiful,' stammered the sweaty businessman.

Haruka looked down at her book and ignored him. He collected his briefcase from between his legs and rose in order to get out at the next stop. He shoved past the crowd in front of them to get to the door and embarrassed Haruka one last time with a final desperate look and the words: 'Please call me.'

Haruka tried to appear engrossed in her English conversation textbook. The bemused middle-aged lady took his seat, still smiling to herself.

Haruka shut her eyes for a while and cringed. A few minutes later, wondering where they were, she opened her eyes again and realised that the carriage was a lot less crowded and she could reach the door without having to push past anyone. She was only a couple of stops from her station. Haruka put her English book back into her bag and standing up, she edged her way to the door, leaving the sweaty man's business card on the seat. Taking her mirror from her bag, she touched up her lips with a rosy Chanel lipgloss and blotted her nose with her powder compact. Happy with her reflection, Haruka adjusted her headband and waited, now impatient to reach her stop at Ōfune, where her car was parked in the station car park.

As Haruka pulled into the driveway and parked her car in front of her house, she decided to go and visit Yuriko, even though it was getting late. She hadn't seen her for a few days, and she missed her. Haruka put the car in park, grabbed her bag and brushed her hair before locking up the car and heading up the long driveway next door.

Mr Makimoto, Yuriko's father, answered the door. He was a man of few words, who always gave the impression of being a very busy person with no time for small talk. After a brief greeting and Haruka removing her shoes at the entrance, he directed her upstairs to Yuriko's bedroom.

Once upstairs, Haruka turned the corner on the landing and was surprised to find Yuriko's chubby younger brother dressed in his school uniform crouching down with his ear pressed to her bedroom door. The naughty look on his face turned red with shame when he saw Haruka looking down at him suspiciously.

'She's upset again. My sister's been crying for over half an hour and I just wanted to check to see if she was all right,' he said to Haruka, trying hard to adopt a look of brotherly concern.

'Well I think you should head back to your own room. Don't you have some homework to do?' Haruka asked him. The kind authority in her voice made him scurry off quickly back to his own room.

Haruka could hear Yuriko's sobs behind the door above the whirring sound of her exercise bike. She knocked gently on the door and the crying stopped, only to be replaced by the sound of her trying to contain her emotions.

Haruka gently opened the door and peeped inside. Yuriko had her back to the door. She was dressed in an oversized T-shirt and jeans and strands of her long lanky hair were clinging on to her sweaty face. Yuriko was dabbing her forehead and blowing her nose with several tissues, cycling frantically, unaware that Haruka was behind her. It upset her to see Yuriko in this state. Haruka called out her name and she turned. Despite a red nose and mascara running down her cheeks, Yuriko attempted a wide smile when she saw it was Haruka coming in to see her, but she continued to cycle as though her legs were disengaged with a maniacal life of their own.

'I'm sorry you have to see me like this,' Yuriko blurted out between her sobs, which had become less dramatic and more controlled. 'I went shopping in Yokohama earlier today, and who do you think I saw there?'

'I don't know,' Haruka replied, sitting down on the edge of the bed. 'I guess you ran into Ryō, because I know he lives in that area and maybe you had an argument.' Yuriko had been dating a boy Haruka had never met called Ryō for about eight weeks, and Haruka had sensed for a while now before today that they had a volatile relationship.

'Good guess, Haruka, and you're half right. I didn't have any plans to meet up with him today, but I was coming out of Sogo Department Store and I saw him walking from the station. I was going to rush up and say hello when I noticed that he wasn't alone.' Yuriko took her hands off the bike handles to blow her nose and wipe the mascara away from under her eyes as she peddled. 'He was with a young, pretty girl about our age. I didn't want to jump to conclusions and get jealous and upset, because I thought she might be his sister or someone like that, so I decided to follow them.'

Haruka crossed her legs and leant forward. 'So you decided to follow them,' she repeated, nodding her head and urging Yuriko to continue.

'Yes,' Yuriko replied. 'I kept my distance so they couldn't see me and they started to head towards Chinatown.'

'Go on,' Haruka said.

'Well, you're not going to believe this, but as they walked through Chinatown, Ryō took the girl's hand, and they walked down the street, both of them looking blissfully happy – and that's when I started to get upset, wondering what my boyfriend was doing behind my back.' Yuriko's face started to contort again and tears started running down her cheeks.

Haruka went over and placed her hand on her shoulder.

'But that's not the worst part,' Yuriko said between gasping sobs. 'I kept following them and of course they didn't see me, because they were so wrapped up in each other, and before long I could see where they were going.'

'Where were they going?' Haruka asked Yuriko, her face incredulous.

'They were going to a love hotel!' Yuriko replied, still peddling like a crazy woman.

'*Noooo*,' Haruka said, now feeling really upset about what Ryō had done to her friend. 'What a sleazy two-timer.' She sat down on the edge of Yuriko's bed.

'Oh, yes – I hate Ryō and I never want to see him again. If he tries to call me, I won't answer and if he sends me a text message, I won't respond to the sleaze.'

'Yes, that's exactly what you should do,' Haruka reassured her. 'Come on, get down off the bike before your legs fall off.'

Yuriko slowly wound down and eventually dropped off the bike and fell onto the bed next to Haruka, curling up into the foetal position. Haruka stood up to give her more room and went over to sit down on the bright pink candy-striped sofa chair opposite, very concerned about her friend.

27

'I'm thinking of buying some laxatives,' said Yuriko, looking at picture of a skeletal girl jumping in the air on the front cover of the magazine at her side.

'You can't do that – laxatives will make you ill,' replied Haruka.

'But I've put on a kilo and I want to lose it quickly. I read on the internet about a girl who lost two kilos in a week just by taking laxatives for a few days.'

'Did you know that you could have a heart attack if you take them for the wrong reason?'

'Don't be silly, Haruka. I'm not going to have a heart attack. You do make me laugh.'

'I'm not joking. Promise me you won't try laxatives or any other weight loss tablets you read about on the internet,' said Haruka, covering her eyes in shock and shaking her head.

'Don't worry, I know what I'm doing,' Yuriko replied, laughing at Haruka's obvious concern. 'I've been taking weight loss pills on and off for six months and I feel fine.'

They sat there in silence for about ten minutes. Yuriko flicked through the magazine in front of her and Haruka looked around the room, searching for any evidence of weight loss pills. She noticed a container beside Yuriko's pillow, but she didn't want to give her another lecture. Haruka decided that her friend needed support, not criticism, so she kept quiet.

Bored with flipping through her magazine, Yuriko sat up and swung her legs over the side of the bed. 'I'll be back in a minute,' she said. 'I just need to use the bathroom.'

'Take your time, Yuriko.'

Haruka sat back and sighed, wishing her good friend had not had to witness this today. Poor Yuriko had been head over heels in love when she'd met Ryō just a few weeks ago. Haruka was happy for her, but concerned about the effect he was having on her self-image. She'd been dieting frantically for some time now and since she'd met Ryō, she'd become even more obsessed with diet and exercise. Haruka could tell that she thought if she just ate a little less each day and exercised frantically, she'd be the perfect woman, just like those models on the cover of the fashion magazines piled up in the corner next to her bed. Haruka wished she could figure out how to stop her friend from continuing to diet when she didn't need to anymore and convince her that she was absolutely fine without this excessive exercising.

Haruka looked around her friend's room, in which she'd spent many hours gossiping and enjoying her company. It was decorated throughout in various shades of pink. She wondered when Yuriko was going to refurbish the room and do away with the cuddly Hello Kitty toys piled up at the head of the bed and the children's books on the bookshelf in the corner that had not been picked up for at least eight years. There were also several magazines on dieting on her pillow, which she'd obviously been researching that evening. This concerned Haruka, but not as much as the pro-anorexia websites she knew she'd been devouring lately.

Haruka turned to see Yuriko came back into the room from her en-suite bathroom a different person, with a controlled and determined face, newly made up with a fresh coat of foundation and mascara.

'Let's change the subject, Haruka. You've just come back from work and you must be exhausted. Tell me, did you meet up with Takashi this evening?'

'Yes we met up in Omotesando again,' Haruka replied, happy to oblige and change the subject.

'How was that?' asked Yuriko, seemingly transformed into an emotionally balanced person compared to the scene only minutes earlier.

'It was great meeting up with him, but I told him about my job offer in Kyoto and he wasn't happy about it. Now I feel a twinge of guilt not telling him how much time I've been spending with your cousin Jun lately.'

'Oh, there's no need to feel guilty about that, Haruka. You aren't dating Takashi seriously yet and you've only met up two or three times with Jun in the last couple of months, and that's only ever been purely innocent. You're just beating yourself up over nothing. You've done nothing wrong,' Yuriko reassured her.

'Thanks, Yuriko,' Haruka replied. 'To tell you the truth, I absolutely adore Takashi and I'd like to take our relationship to the next level, but I'm afraid I might be making a mistake if I do that and I know this would upset my mother – you know how much she likes Jun.'

'Yes I do,' replied Yuriko. 'Is it because she likes him or his money?'

'I'm really not sure,' said Haruka. 'Well, if you're feeling better now, I better head home. My parents will be wondering where I am.' Haruka picked up her handbag.

'Okay thanks, Haruka,' said Yuriko. 'Don't forget Jun will be staying here again Sunday week and he'll probably want to see you that evening.'

'I haven't forgotten,' Haruka replied as she stood up to leave. 'By the way, did you know your younger brother had his ear to the door earlier, listening to you when you were upset?'

'I didn't realise he was doing that again. He gets bored because he has no one to talk to most of the time. You know what my parents are like. My mother's always socialising and my father's too busy with work.'

Haruka thought about this and how rarely she saw Yuriko's father. He was the general manager of an import/export company and one of those salary men who rarely came home.

'As well as this, you know my family are lucky if we see my brother at home more than twice a week in the evening and I'm always busy or at the gym, so he's been inventing ways to keep himself amused,' said Yuriko. 'I'll have a word with him tomorrow.'

There was a knock on Yuriko's bedroom door. Her older brother Taroo poked his head through and jiggled his car keys at the girls.

'We were just talking about you,' said Yuriko.

'All good, I hope,' he said to them, flashing Haruka a smile. 'I'm ready to leave for Yokohama. I've just spoken to our cousin and he said he was looking forward to seeing you. You said you wanted to come with me, but it doesn't look like you're ready. Are you coming or not, Yuriko?'

'I never said anything about going with you to Yokohama,' Yuriko replied.

'You told me an hour ago not to leave without you,' said Taroo, not smiling anymore and looking annoyed.

'I don't remember that,' said Yuriko. She stood and whispered to Haruka, 'I love infuriating my brother. He needs to be brought down a peg – he's so full of himself.'

'You're impossible,' hissed Taroo and shut the door behind him with a bang before stomping downstairs in a huff.

'I better go, Yuriko,' said Haruka, quite amused by her neighbour's sibling rivalry. It was not the first time she'd seen Yuriko and Taroo have a go at each other, and it always made her think how nice it would be to have a brother or sister. 'Call me tomorrow,' Haruka said to Yuriko as she headed for the bedroom door.

'Okay Haruka,' her friend replied. 'I promise I'll call you at about eight p.m., after you finish work.'

Haruka had no doubt that she'd call. Yuriko never played games with their friendship. But it wasn't her friendship with Yuriko that worried her. For the next few days, Haruka would be consumed by thoughts of how she might tell Takashi about Jun. She almost rang him a number of times, wanting to blurt out everything and lose the burden weighing heavily on her heart. But each time she stopped herself, believing that time might solve all her problems.

Chapter 3

You must look where it is not
as well as where it is

Returning to his apartment in Kawasaki, Takashi was oblivious to the office workers packed tightly around him. He was still thinking of Haruka and her plans to move to Kyoto and her wanting to take up a management position there at one of the Kansai branches of the English conversation school for which she worked. He decided that he needed to spend some more time with her that month, apart from their regular Thursday night coffees. The fact that she was considering a position on the other side of the country made him want to see her so much more, and he knew that from October, he would have to knuckle down and commit even more to his studies.

On the train back, Takashi decided that he'd call her in the next couple of days and ask her if she'd spend the day with him the following Sunday in Kamakura. This place would be cooler than Tokyo at this time of the year and it was only a short trip for Haruka from her home in Ōfune.

He'd always liked Kamakura, with its Buddhist temples and statues – and compared to the rush and madness of inner Tokyo, it was a place that offered up for him a certain peace and tranquillity. Because of this, it provided value for the young and old alike, especially for those that lived and worked in the concrete jungles of the inner urban cities.

He thought back to when he'd first met Haruka nearly three years ago at university, when he'd sat by her side in a Marketing lecture. His interest in her started on the first day of university when he'd spotted her sitting at the back of the lecture room by herself, searching in her bag for a pen. He clearly remembered her wearing a tight white top that showed off her form. He'd casually wandered over and taken the seat to her right. He wasn't sure at the time if it was the way she flicked her hair back or the scent of her light perfume that attracted him, but he was transfixed by her almost immediately.

Takashi hadn't taken in one word from the lecturer that day, and he'd left the lecture hall without any notes at all, but that didn't matter to him one bit because he'd only been concerned about getting Haruka's phone number at the end of the class. Luckily, when he'd asked for her number she'd agreed to give it to him with a smile – and what a smile! As he got to know her better, he noticed she was always attentive and conscientious in her classes and she was basically a really nice girl, which added to her appeal. Ten months later, he'd been so disappointed when she'd dropped out of university, but he'd respected her reason for doing so.

Haruka was an only child and her father had become very ill at the end of her first year at university. Both mother and daughter had looked after him and had catered to his every whim; there had been much to do. Her parents were fine, respectable people and Haruka had always been very close to them. Her father had suffered from a heart attack. It had been a terrible strain on both Haruka and her mother, but he'd made a full recovery. During this period, Takashi had stayed in touch with Haruka and he'd often spoken to her on the phone.

A few years ago, Takashi had only been thinking of partying with his friends. After he'd met Haruka, she'd made a big impact on him and he'd started to take life a lot more seriously. Haruka had developed from a young girl into a wise woman that her mother had been able to completely depend upon.

Even after her father had recovered, it was a long time before Takashi had been able to meet Haruka in person. But just over a month ago, Haruka had applied for work in the accounts division of an English language school. She'd been assigned to a branch in Harajuku and after this she had been able to meet him at the coffee shop Café hors et dans in Omotesando every week.

During the time that Haruka had been busy helping her mother and looking after her father, Takashi had dated a series of different girls from university. Most of them had been slightly alternative in their thinking and style of dress, and he'd enjoyed being seen with them in front of his buddies. But not one of these girls had interested him as much as Haruka. Despite the fact that he'd liked the ultra-short skirts or revealing dresses on the other girls, he'd also felt that their minds were empty and their hearts were hollow.

Three weeks after Takashi had started meeting Haruka on a regular basis, it had been easy to decide to only meet with her and leave the other girls for his mates at university to have fun with.

Takashi got off his train at Kawasaki. He'd chosen to live in Kawasaki not only because it was such a convenient area in which to live, but also because it had become a really up and coming town over the past few years. The station's plaza and the shops surrounding the area that led up to his apartment provided everything that one could need. He would most often take the east exit at the train station, as this was the most direct exit to reach his home and from there, he could check out the shops in the Marui or Be department stores or sit and enjoy a coffee at the Doutour coffee house. Sometimes he would drop in for a MOS Burger just outside the station. He'd also at one time or another contemplated joining the new and modern gym that he always passed just before he reached his apartment, but somehow he'd always talked himself out of that.

If Takashi didn't want to study some afternoons, he would occasionally wander around the shops that he could reach if he took the west exit. This area had recently been refurbished into a rotunda-style complex full of the trendiest boutiques. There was often a band playing in the courtyard and after he'd looked through most of the four levels of shops, it was nice to just sit and listen to the music. He would take time out there; enjoying a cigarette and watching the people pass by. Some days, if he was on his way into Tokyo and he had twenty or thirty minutes to spare before catching his train, he'd enjoy a lunchbox of fresh specialty dumplings for ¥500 or stand and slurp down a delicious bowl of hot ramen soup with a crowd of other commuters at one of the vendors inside the station above the platforms. His favourite soup was Chashu ramen, with three large pieces of thickly sliced pork floating on a bed of noodles.

That afternoon, Takashi walked slowly to his apartment, situated about ten minutes from the station. He bypassed all the shops and only stopped at the convenience store to buy some ready-made sushi and a cold can of oolong tea.

Takashi had moved to this part of town because his parents lived in Yokosuka. A few years ago, he'd convinced them that it was too far for him to travel to university from there. His parents would be considered neither rich nor poor. His father had worked as a mid-level salary man at a transportation company in Yokosuka for over twenty years. He grew up provided with all the essentials, but when he was younger, his mother had never bought him the latest designer clothes and they'd never been able to afford overseas holidays.

There were a few happy memories he fondly looked back on. He remembered the times his parents had taken him to Hokkaido to visit his mother's side of the family, and they'd also paid for him to go with the rest of his school mates one year on a school trip to Kyoto, which he'd really enjoyed. When he'd been offered a place at a reasonable university a few years ago, his parents had been very proud of him and they'd generously offered to pay his rent while he was studying so that he wouldn't have to commute long distances to get to his lectures and home again. They even gave him a humble weekly allowance. Takashi was extremely grateful for his apartment and it was his very own six-by-ten foot cosy little kingdom.

As Takashi approached the stairs leading up to the first floor landing and his front door, a bicycle stem that someone had thrown onto the guttering above him caught his eye, as it had many times before this month. Lowering his gaze, he noticed that the caretaker for his building was standing outside his apartment and Takashi thought that it was as good a time as any to ask him to remove the bike part that was hanging precariously above him.

'Hey caretaker, do you have time to take this bike stem off the guttering? It's been there for over a month now,' Takashi yelled.

'Can't you see that I'm busy, boy?' he shouted back. 'I've got a list of other things to do before I can fix the guttering.'

'Okay, sorry to bother you,' Takashi said, a bit taken back. He rushed towards his flat, wishing he hadn't said a word to the caretaker.

Takashi's place was small, even by Japanese standards. He liked it like that. He felt cocooned from the outside world, but not isolated. His apartment was in a block of about twenty other similar-sized units. The door was heavy, with a double lock, and inside was a single bed, a little fridge, a Sony TV, a Panasonic stereo and a Toshiba PC– he'd wanted an Apple iMac, but he'd decided it was too expensive. Takashi was a bit of a brand snob when he bought any kind of technology. His room also contained a mini cooker, a toaster, a Panasonic microwave and a kotatsu. Of course he didn't use the kotatsu in this weather, but this coffee table enveloped in a futon, with a heater attached underneath to keep his knees warm, was invaluable in winter. Only the bathroom was separate from everything else in this small apartment. Less to clean, he always told himself.

Attached to the apartment, there was also a balcony where he kept his washing machine and above this, a plastic frame with twelve pastel blue pegs for drying his clothes after the wash. This area was so small that only one person could stand and look out over dozens of other apartments with washing machines and freshly washed clothes.

Until a couple of years ago, he'd also had a Microsoft Xbox 360 and thirty-seven games to go with it. That had kept him busy most of the time, but that interest came to a sudden end the first time Haruka visited him at his apartment at the end of the first three months at university. He'd spent an hour showing her how easily he could get through the first five stages of one particular game when she'd pressed the power button deleting all his efforts after a solid hour of impressive playing. She'd told him that it had been the most boring sixty minutes she'd ever spent with him. On an impulse the following day, he'd sold the console and every one of the games.

The first three months without his Xbox were difficult as he tried to find different ways of filling up his spare time and he even considered buying the games back on several occasions, but he soon found out that his studies were improving without the distraction and his friends Masaya and Kenji were happy to hear the last of his conversations about his Xbox abilities.

Takashi sat down, turned on the TV and settled down to watch a game show. He glanced at his textbooks piled up in the corner of the room. He felt like those books were staring at him and trying to make him feel guilty for neglecting them. He took his jacket off the bed and threw it over them. Now that they were out of view, he knew he'd be able to ignore any urge to study.

He'd just about finished his sushi when he received a phone call from his cousin Katsuro, who lived in Yōga.

'Hi Takashi, it's Katsuro. How're you doing?' he asked.

'Fine, thanks, good to hear from you,' Takashi replied. 'What's new?'

'Not a lot. Sorry I haven't spoken to you recently. I've been really busy at work.'

'You have the best job, don't you? I know you work really hard, but you get a lot of perks working for such a prestigious trading company,' said Takashi.

'Wait and see, Takashi. When you begin to work, you'll understand that my job sounds a lot better than it actually is.'

Takashi lit a cigarette. 'How's Mika?' he asked, flicking his ash into the ashtray.

'She's okay thanks.'

'And the house?' asked Takashi. 'Are you enjoying living at this new place in Yōga?'

'I miss Australia and being able to walk to the beach on the weekends. My house was also a lot bigger over there.'

Takashi put his hand to his mouth and coughed before stubbing out the end of the cigarette. 'But this house in Yōga is nice, isn't it?' Takashi asked with his hand to his mouth.

'What did you say?' asked Katsuro.

'Sorry, I have a tickle in my throat. Your home – it's nice, isn't it?'

'Well, yes,' said Katsuro. 'It's much smaller, but Mika's happy because she missed Tokyo and now she doesn't have as much to clean.'

'You know I wanted to visit you in Australia, but I couldn't afford the plane ticket. Will you be going back there?'

'No, I don't think so. I think I'll be posted in London within the next two years.'

'For how long?' Takashi asked.

'It will probably be a four-year stint, but I'd prefer to go back to Australia. Hey Takashi, why don't you come to visit us next Saturday? We live about five minutes from Yōga train station. Will you come for dinner?'

'I can't make it this Saturday because I have to go and visit my grandmother in Yokosuka, but are you free the following Saturday?' Takashi asked.

'Sure, that would be fine, Takashi.'

'By the way, what's Mika planning on making for dinner?'

Takashi knew Mika was an excellent cook and he always looked forward to her meals.

Katsuro laughed. 'I don't know yet. Does it matter?'

'Of course not! I'll be there about six p.m. if that suits you. Can you e-mail me the directions?'

'Sure. See you then, Takashi.'

'Bye, Katsuro.'

He hadn't seen Katsuro for a few years. He was the eldest son of his mother's brother, and he was just as much a close friend as he was his cousin. When they were younger, he'd been someone that Takashi and his older brother had really respected. The time that Katsuro had spent with Takashi when his brother had passed away was so generous of him that it was something that would always be appreciated and never forgotten. Although Katsuro had been busy with his university exams at the time, he would often visit Takashi's family in Yokosuka and sit with his parents or take him outside to play baseball or help Takashi to practise the art of Kendo. He'd always been a much better sportsman than Takashi, but he would often let him win at games just to cheer him up when Katsuro knew that he was having a difficult time.

Katsuro had met his wife Mika a couple of years after he'd started working at the trading company he'd joined after his graduation. She'd been a secretary there. According to Katsuro, they'd hit it off almost immediately, and three years ago they'd married. When Takashi had first met Mika, he thought that she was very demure and painfully shy, but as he got to know her better, they'd became more comfortable with each other and now he really enjoyed seeing her because she was extremely nice and often a lot of fun. Takashi was really looking forward to next week. He'd never had a bad meal at his cousin's house and the food was always as good as their company.

Takashi's phone beeped and vibrated in the palm of his hand. A smile crept onto his face when he saw that it was Haruka's name that flashed up onto the screen. She must have called while he was on the phone to Katsuro. He checked to see if she'd left a voice message, but she hadn't.

He dialled her number. He didn't even hear the ring tone. Haruka must have been waiting for the call.

'Moshi moshi,' said Haruka on the other end of the phone. She sounded happy that he'd returned her call.

'You just called me, Haruka?' Takashi said to her, wiping his beaded forehead with the back of his left hand. The combination of Haruka's voice and the heat and the humidity in his apartment were dramatically increasing his body temperature.

'I just called to thank you for tonight.'

'My pleasure,' Takashi replied.

'Did you have a good time?' she asked.

Takashi's smile broadened. 'Definitely. Um … Haruka, what are you doing Sunday week?'

'Nothing during the day. Some friends might be coming over on that Sunday night,' she said.

Takashi was about to ask who they were, but he stopped himself. 'Would you like to spend the day with me in Kamakura?'

'Sounds good. By the way, I can't meet you next Thursday. I just remembered that I have to work late.'

'Not to worry – I'll see you the following Sunday,' Takashi said to her. 'How about I meet you at Kamakura station at ten a.m.?'

'Okay that sounds good,' said Haruka. 'Thanks again for this evening.'

Takashi was about to reply when the floor suddenly started shaking underneath him. The empty sushi container and chopsticks on the table in front of him fell onto the carpet. He dropped his mobile phone as he tried to stand up.

'Are you there?' cried out Haruka on the other end of the line.

He could hear Haruka calling out to him as he grabbed his phone as well as his keys and his jacket, ready for an emergency exit from his apartment.

'Sorry, the room is shaking … it's an earthquake – can you feel it?' Takashi asked Haruka.

'No, I can't feel a thing,' she replied.

'Well, you are quite far away … wait a minute, it seems all right now … I think it has stopped,' said Takashi.

'Are you going to be okay?' Haruka asked him.

'I'll be fine. I'd better go. I'll call you in the next few days.'

'Okay. I'm looking forward to hearing from you. Bye, Takashi.'

'Bye, Haruka,' Takashi replied. He put down the phone. It annoyed him that the recent earthquakes seemed like they were constantly interrupting any quality communication he was hoping to have with Haruka. There were no more tremors to follow and Haruka filled his thoughts as he cleaned up the container and chopsticks that had fallen onto the carpet. He had constantly kept in touch with her by phone for quite a few years. He'd been so concerned about her when her father was ill that he couldn't help but call her on a regular basis.

This telephone tennis gave him the opportunity to try and lift her spirits, and before long, it also had a positive effect on him. Now, if they didn't talk for up to three days, he really missed her and it felt like something was lacking in his life. This feeling would only subside if he spoke to her again. He decided it was going to be a long week waiting for the following weekend when he could spend more time with her, especially with the tedious visit to his grandmother in the next couple of days.

CHAPTER 4

By companying with the wise,
a man shall learn wisdom

It was over a week later, at four p.m. on Saturday, when Takashi disembarked from the train at Shibuya. From there, he changed platforms to take the Tōkyū Den-en-toshi line to Yōga. The rainy season was still upon them. It was very wet outside and the air was moist. There had only been a smattering of showers earlier that day, but now it was raining heavily.

Because the afternoon air was still incredibly humid, his linen shirt that was so crisp and clean only an hour earlier was now wet and sticking to his chest. He knew that the heat would continue like this for another couple of months before the cool autumn breezes descended on Tokyo.

Takashi took his seat on the train bound for Yōga and checked his mobile phone for messages. His mother had sent him a text telling him how good it had been to see him the previous weekend and how she'd been impressed with his patience as he'd listened for over two hours to his grandmother's various grumbles and grievances. Takashi sent her a message back to let her know that he was looking forward to seeing her and his father again soon. This was not untrue. Although Takashi liked the independence he had living in Kawasaki, it had been an easy and enjoyable life growing up in Yokosuka. His mother had always been strict, yet kind, and his father had always been very easy going – he was the joker in the house. When Takashi's brother died and he and his mother had been completely distraught, it was his father who had carried them through this difficult time. His father had never allowed them to continue to carry the burden of his brother's death, and his lighthearted manner had helped them to extinguish a lot of the pain.

Takashi's train pulled into Yōga station and he ascended up and out past the exit and into the street. Although he'd been to Yōga a couple of times before, this would be the first time he'd visited his cousin's house there. They'd settled here in the spring. Katsuro and his wife had just recently returned from a two-year working stint in Australia and Katsuro's company had provided them with this lovely house when they'd returned to Japan. It was a very convenient location for them, as it was close to the parks and shops in the neighbouring town of Futako-Tamagawa. Yōga was also a very respectable town in the district of Setagaya, and because of its proximity to central Tokyo, it was an enviable place in which to live.

Takashi checked the e-mail his cousin had sent him with the directions to his house and walked the two blocks from the station to his home. He rang the doorbell at their pretty brick entrance. It was surrounded by rose bushes drooping in the rain.

Katsuro's wife Mika answered the door and Takashi greeted her with a big smile.

'My dear Takashi,' she said. 'Come on inside. You're soaking wet.'

'Yes, it's been raining pretty heavily,' he replied.

She pulled the door open wide to allow him into the entrance of the house. Takashi gave Mika a friendly bow as he removed his jacket and shoes and slid into the house slippers she provided.

'It's been a while since I've seen you, Mika.'

'Yes,' she replied. 'How've you been?'

'Good – very good, in fact,' Takashi said. He handed Mika a present he'd brought for her and Katsuro. It was a box of cakes filled with sweetened red bean-paste made from azuki beans.

'Thank you, Takashi, that's very nice of you,' said Mika as she took the gift from him. 'Well, come on inside. Katsuro has been really looking forward to seeing you again.'

Takashi followed Mika into the living room. Her hair was pulled back into a bun, and she was wearing a long apron that covered her cotton shirt and knee-length skirt. Her clothes were simple in their design, but obviously expensive.

Mika called out to Katsuro to come downstairs as Takashi sat down in an extremely comfortable sofa in their small but beautifully furnished living room. There was a delicious smell of homemade Japanese dishes coming from the kitchen. Katsuro came down the stairs and Mika scurried away to finish preparing the meal.

Katsuro was thirty-three years old, but he had the boyish grin of someone in his mid-twenties. He held out his hand to Takashi as he bounded across the living room, and Takashi instantly felt relaxed and at home. Katsuro was wearing a Ralph Lauren blue polo shirt and indigo denim jeans. Mika brought in a couple of Kirin beers and Katsuro poured both of them a glass.

'It's good to see you again,' he said.

'Yes,' Takashi replied, taking a sip of his beer. 'It's been a long time.'

'So what have you been up to?' Katsuro asked Takashi.

'Well, I've been studying a lot.'

'And how's that been going?'

'Not too bad.'

'And how are your mother and father, Takashi?'

'They're well, I went to see them last weekend and we visited my grandmother. Do you remember meeting her at my brother's funeral?'

'Yes, I've met her a few times. She always seemed nice, but very reserved and quite strict. I would even say I remember her as being a bit intimidating.'

4 4

'Yes that's my grandmother,' Takashi said.

'Does she live close to your parents in Yokosuka?'

'Yes, it takes about an hour to drive to her house. I have to tell you, I think she was not her usual self last week. We arrived at her house at about four p.m. and we sat in the tatami room as usual. While my mother was making us all tea, my grandmother spent quite a long time relaying her usual gripes. She talked about the young people of today losing touch with the real Japan. How girls' skirts were too short; their hair was not supposed to be blonde and that too many of them were unnecessarily promiscuous. She also complained about the fact that the youth of Japan were all getting too fat from eating too much Western fast food and that young men were driving way too fast in their modified cars,' Takashi said, pausing to take a long sip of his beer, after which Katsuro refilled his glass.

'Go on,' said Katsuro, amused by this portrayal of Takashi's grandmother.

'When my mother brought the tea into the room, my grandmother started asking me questions she'd never asked before,' said Takashi.

'Such as?' asked Katsuro.

'Well, she asked me about my studies and whether I had a girlfriend or not. She even asked me how many children I'd like, when I plan to get married and whether I plan to live in Tokyo in the future or further afield.'

'What's wrong with that? It sounds like she was being nice.'

'That's the strange part about it. My grandmother has never been that friendly.'

'What did your parents say about this?'

'They told me not to worry about it.'

'Maybe your grandmother is just softening in her old age,' said Katsuro.

'Yes, you're probably right,' Takashi replied.

Katsuro poured him another beer and Takashi started telling him about his hopes to work at one of the major trading companies. Soon after, without him realising it, he started talking about Haruka.

'I think Haruka's the one I'd like to marry one day,' he told his cousin.

'Is she pretty, Takashi?' asked Katsuro.

'Oh, very pretty,' he replied. 'But I'm worried I'll never be able to date her because I'm not sure whether she feels the same way about me. I think she might be seeing an ex-boyfriend again and she's talking about taking a job in Kyoto.'

Katsuro laughed. 'What a person says and thinks is not always how they feel, Takashi.'

Mika must have heard them talking about Haruka from the kitchen. She leaned around the kitchen door and called out to Takashi. 'Be careful, Takashi, a beautiful rose may have many thorns.'

'Yes, I think one of your thorns scratched me earlier,' replied her husband. They all laughed.

Takashi really liked Katsuro because he was always positive and a very good listener. He always felt that he was learning something from him, particularly how he should converse with others without being intrusive. Takashi somehow felt that this could be a great asset in the future.

They finished two more glasses of Kirin beer before Mika brought some of the dishes to the table for them to start eating. Mika didn't eat much during the dinner. She kept going back and forth from the kitchen to the table, always bringing in another array of food. Takashi felt honoured to enjoy such a feast. Before him was a selection of his favourite dishes: Chilled tofu, yakiniku pork marinated in soy sauce, garlic, ginger and sugar, an assortment of vegetables and the obligatory steamed rice and miso soup. Mika was obviously delighted by the smiles on their faces every time another favourite dish arrived.

After dinner, Katsuro and Mika talked about their experiences in Australia.

'What was the house like over there? Was it really a lot bigger?' Takashi asked them.

'Oh, it was huge. It had three levels and the kitchen was four times bigger than the one I cook in here,' Mika said.

'How about golf, Katsuro? Did you play a lot of golf?' asked Takashi.

'Every weekend – but I'm still not very good. The golf courses were magnificent though – they stretched for miles.'

'Did you eat a lot of beef and Western food?'

'Well, Mika made mostly Japanese food at home. They have Japanese grocery stores there. But when we went out to eat, I would always order a steak,' said Katsuro. He showed Takashi the width of the Australian steaks by indicating with his index finger and his thumb.

They talked a lot more about Australia that evening. Mika told Takashi about the koalas and the kangaroos that she'd seen close up, as well as the English classes that she'd attended once a week. She explained to him how she had hoped to speak more English when she was living there, but she'd mostly spent her free time with other Japanese ladies. Apparently they'd all met for lunch in various Japanese restaurants once a month. Takashi was surprised to hear that there were so many Japanese restaurants in Australia and that you could buy take-away sushi from many vendors scattered around town.

Katsuro spoke about how wide the roads were, even in the centre of the major cities. He also talked about the Australian people with whom he'd worked. He admired the way they could speak so frankly and the generous hospitality he had received from them.

Takashi's eyes were wide open and he was captivated as he'd never heard of such things. He told them that in the future he, too, would like to go to Australia, Europe or America.

Later that night, Katsuro and Takashi sat down in the living room and started to drink a little sake. At first, Katsuro spoke with even more enthusiasm about

Australia and its culture, but as the evening progressed and the sake loosened his lips, Katsuro spoke in more serious tones.

Katsuro explained how Mika had become increasingly withdrawn over the past two years. When they'd married three years ago, she'd always been positive and outgoing, but Takashi's cousin explained that she was losing her spirit of late and there was only one reason for it.

'Mika's thirty-two years old now, and for three years she's been trying to have a baby, but she hasn't been able to get pregnant. She won't say anything, but she's not as happy as she used to be,' explained Katsuro.

He went on to tell Takashi that many of the wives of his colleagues that were working for the same trading company in Australia would often meet to keep themselves entertained. Most of the older women over thirty had children and Mika was desperate for a little one of her own.

Being younger than Katsuro and not as worldly, Takashi could only listen and assure him that they would definitely have a child in the future. He truly believed that Mika would be a wonderful mother one day.

Mika came back downstairs and into the room where they were sitting. Both Katsuro and Takashi were quite sloshed from the beer and the sake. She came to tell Takashi that he must stay the night and there was no way he could go home at that hour.

Takashi slept on a futon in their tatami room set out especially for him. His stomach was full and his head was awash with liquor. He soon fell into a strange and vivid dream. It was springtime and he was walking along a street that he did not recognise. There were people having picnics all along the side of the road under the cherry blossom trees. Suddenly, he saw Haruka and he began running towards her, but the faster he tried to run, the further away she appeared. Somehow he tripped and the ground began to shake. The petals from the cherry blossoms fell on him and around him, smothering his entire body. They kept falling and soon he was covered in so many petals, he could no longer see Haruka. He tried to brush off the petals, but it was all in vain. He started sinking and spiralling further into the darkness and then suddenly Takashi woke up with a thud. It was probably about six a.m., judging from the light at the window.

Takashi looked around the room. On one side was a small family Buddhist altar with an incense burner and holder, Buddhist tableware, a candlestick, a bell and flowers for the souls of deceased ancestors. On the facing wall was a print. The print was of a single stem of a cherry blossom branch. He hadn't noticed this the night before. It must have been because of the beer and the sake. Takashi went back to sleep and slept well before he left to go home in the morning.

CHAPTER 5

He that would the daughter
win must the mother first begin

On Sunday morning, Takashi prepared for his trip to Kamakura to meet Haruka. He woke early at seven a.m., had a cold shower and shaved carefully. He even took out a ruler to measure his sideburns before he left just to make sure they were perfectly straight and aligned. The sky was clearer today and it did not look like it would rain; yet the humidity was still extremely high. He picked up a new navy T-shirt that he'd purchased at Seibu department store in Shibuya the week before and pulled it over his head, enjoying the feel of new cotton. After pulling up his pair of khaki shorts that fell below his knees and were covered in pockets, he looked for a pair of clean socks. He could only find one fresh pair with a rather large hole in the foot of the left sock. Not worrying about that, he pulled them on along with his running shoes. He felt fresh and confident as he headed towards the station.

At Shin-Kawasaki station, Takashi bought a can of Coke and a packet of Mild Seven cigarettes from the vending machines on the platform. It wasn't long before the train arrived. As it was Sunday, the trains were quite crowded with families on day trips. He boarded the first carriage. He often did this on longer trips, so that he could watch the train driver and the view ahead. When Takashi was a child, he'd always thought that train drivers and taxi drivers were not human but some kind of mechanical robots. They always wore clean, formal uniforms complemented by spotless white gloves and official caps. Their expressions were set and they always sat rigidly as they moved the controls.

He stood for a while and watched the driver and the scenery stream by as the train picked up speed and then smoothly slowed down at each station, over and over again. Finally, the heat of the day forced him to sit down and wait with the others on board. He could see that everyone was wishing that the next stop would be his or her destination. There was no air-conditioning on this train.

At last, the train pulled into Kamakura at nine fifty a.m. Takashi came out of the station and found Haruka there waiting for him.

'Hi, you look fresh,' he said to her.

'I haven't been on a long train journey. Did it take you ages to get here?' asked Haruka.

'Only about ninety minutes,' Takashi replied.

'Ninety minutes! Did you have air-conditioning on the train?'

'No, and it was really stuffy because there were so many people on my carriage.' Takashi wiped the sweat from his brow. 'Did you drive here?' he asked her.

'Yes, I parked the car near the station,' she said, pointing to the adjoining car park.

'So you did buy a car. What did you end up getting, Haruka?'

'A Nissan March,' she replied.

'That's a perfect car for you,' Takashi said. He could picture Haruka in this curvy "handbag car".

Takashi knew a lot about this town, as he'd visited often. Many people regarded Kamakura to be the Kyoto of the east. It is situated in the Kanagawa prefecture. Hundreds of years ago, it was the political centre of Japan. These days, it's a renowned tourist destination, with many historical monuments, shrines and temples.

Haruka and Takashi decided to walk around Kamakura, rather than drive. He thought that she looked lovely. She was wearing a white A-line linen dress and her hair was tied back casually in a ponytail. The effect of the dress swinging from one side to the other as she walked and the style of her hair gave her a much younger appearance today.

They chatted as they walked.

'Where did you go to primary school, Haruka?'

'In Ōfune,' she replied. 'But I didn't like that school.'

'Can you tell me why?'

'I was really tiny until the age of twelve and the kids used to tease me and tell me my head was too big for my body. I don't know why I'm telling you this. I don't usually talk about it to anyone.'

'You're not going to believe this, but I had a similar problem,' said Takashi. 'I was so small and the other boys in primary school used to rough me up a bit because I wasn't big enough to defend myself.' Takashi shuddered as he remembered the bruises the young boys used to inflict on him. 'But when I was fourteen, I had this amazing growth spurt and now I'm quite tall because of it.'

'I can understand exactly how you feel,' said Haruka.

Takashi and Haruka gazed at each other with a knowing smile. It was times like this that Takashi knew that they were meant to be together. They had so much in common.

Takashi thought it was a good time to change the subject. He didn't want Haruka to harbour any bad memories. 'How's your father, Haruka?' Takashi asked her, knowing that he was much better than he used to be. Waiting for a response, Takashi took out his packet of cigarettes and lit one up. He started puffing as they gazed at the lush landscape surrounding the temples.

'He's a lot better now,' said Haruka with a smile.

Takashi blew the smoke from his cigarette away from her.

'And your parents, Takashi ... how are they?' Haruka asked.

'Both well, father's still working a lot. He doesn't get home until about eleven p.m., and every night my mother waits for him and has his dinner prepared when he walks in the door.'

'Just like my mother used to do,' Haruka said.

'Well, now that your father is retired, he doesn't eat late, does he? Wouldn't he eat with you and your mother now?'

'Yes,' she replied.

'How much older is your father than your mother, Haruka?'

Haruka adjusted her hair clip. 'Fifteen years older.'

'What does he do now that he doesn't work and he's feeling better?' Takashi asked.

'He really tries to keep himself busy. I think he misses going into the office and sometimes irritates my mother when he has nothing to do. He goes to the golf range a lot or reads books. He also likes cable television. He can sit for hours watching wildlife documentaries.'

'That's sweet,' Takashi said.

'Yes, I suppose you're right,' Haruka said with a smile.

Despite the heat, there were many tourists in Kamakura that Sunday. They saw a lot of foreigners: tall Americans chatting with great enthusiasm, stocky Germans showing great interest in the temples, and many others speaking in languages they did not recognise. They also heard the relaxed accent from the Kansai area of Japan. It seemed to Takashi that the older these western Japanese people were, the less likely they were to disguise their rural language and accents. This set them apart from the Tokyo people and the Tokyo dialect. He almost envied them, these elderly country folk who still lived in a past world, where they had no reason to impress or imitate others.

They visited many temples, but Haruka liked the Zen garden behind the Kenchoji Temple the most. They breathed in the serenity and calmness of the place. It was fifteen minutes before they decided to keep walking. They headed south towards the Great Buddha, a bronze statue over thirteen metres in height. It didn't take them long to get there. They walked up the steps to the base and marvelled at its vastness.

'This statue of Kotokuri, commonly called the Daibutsu,' Takashi explained to Haruka, 'was first made of wood, but is now constructed from bronze. It's the largest Buddha in Kamakura.'

'Really! I didn't know that it was originally made of wood,' she replied with interest.

They gazed upon the fresh flowers and fruit that had been placed in front of the Great Buddha. His eyes were lowered in prayer; his hands held together in contemplation.

At one fifteen p.m., they headed back to where Haruka had parked her car, the Nissan March, near the station. From there, they drove along the coast of Sagami Bay towards Enoshima Island.

'This island is where the Samurai used to pray during times of battle or reflect on their teachings during the Edo Period,' Haruka told Takashi in the car on the way. He was pleased that she, too, shared an appreciation of Japanese culture and history.

They found a convenient car park on the island and headed up the steep steps to the Enoshima shrine. Many people had come to receive blessings.

They paid their respects at the three temples at the top of the stairs and having done so, they turned to head back.

'I heard that many people come to this island to ask for blessings for special occasions, such as marriages or births,' said Haruka, descending down the steps from the shrine.

Little did she know that moments earlier, Takashi had silently offered his own prayer at the shrine that one day he would have the chance to marry Haruka.

Starting to feel hungry, they decided to head back to Kamakura to eat a late lunch at a popular soba noodle restaurant. They found a restaurant of Haruka's choice and went inside to find a few couples and three families with small children. They both ordered chilled Zaru soba noodles and Takashi started telling Haruka about his stay in Yōga at his cousin Katsuro's house. He proudly described the pretty house and Mika's expert cooking. He deliberately left out the part about their desire to have children and the problems they were having in his explanation.

As usual, Haruka was very attentive. Takashi also marvelled at the way she withstood the incredible humidity. He was so proud to be sitting next to such a beautiful girl who could listen to him so politely and give him her full attention.

When Haruka laughed, her cheeks would turn pink, her eyes would light up and her shoulders would shake a little. Unlike a lot of other girls, she would not place her hand over her mouth to hide her smile or her teeth. It was like she really enjoyed laughing. She enthralled him.

'Are you still taking English lessons, Haruka?' Takashi asked her as the waitress handed them their noodles.

'Yes, every week,' she replied.

'Are you fluent in the language?' Takashi asked with a mouth full of noodles.

'No, far from it, although I've been taking classes every week for about three years, I wouldn't say that I was at all fluent.'

'Where did you take the lessons before you started working at the English School in Harajuku?'

'I used to go to an English conversation school in Yokohama when my father was ill. It was the only time I'd ever leave the house, but it was really good for me because I needed to get out sometimes.'

'I studied English grammar in junior high school, but I find that English pronunciation is the most difficult part of learning the language,' Takashi said to her.

'I've just got my tongue around pronouncing the *'th'* sound,' said Haruka. 'Try and say *'thank you'*, Takashi.'

'*Zank you*,' he said.

Haruka bent over with laughter. 'Put your tongue between your teeth when you say it. Try again.'

'*Thank you*,' Takashi said perfectly, for the first time ever.

'Very good,' she replied.

They spent the next few minutes smiling at each other. Takashi was sure that he shared an energy with Haruka that set them apart from other couples. He wished that he could repeat that day over and over, so that he could savour the hours he was spending with her.

'Have you heard anything more about the management position in Kyoto?' Takashi asked her, hoping she'd tell him she'd changed her mind about taking the job.

'They want me to go out to Kyoto for an interview next week.'

'Oh, that's good for you,' he replied unenthusiastically. 'Is it going to be a permanent position?'

'Yes, it is. Takashi, I understand if you'd prefer me to stay in Tokyo,' she said, sensing his disappointment. 'I love Tokyo and I really enjoy seeing you regularly. I'll miss you when I move to Kyoto.'

'And I'll really miss you, too,' said Takashi. 'Your father said on the phone you've been meeting up with your ex-boyfriend from Kyoto.' He thought this was a good time to mention him.

'Yes, Takashi,' she replied, looking down at her noodles. 'We've been out a few times ... but I don't think it's serious.'

Takashi couldn't see her eyes, and wondered why she didn't look straight up at him when she said this. He wanted so much to continue this conversation, but his throat was dry and his brain wouldn't allow him to articulate the words. He knew that if he stuttered and spluttered out a response, he would sound accusing and this would be inappropriate. The rest of the meal was eaten in silence. Takashi was obviously uncomfortable and Haruka felt the same. She looked up now and then and gave him the kind of smile a teacher would give a student struggling to learn a new subject. It was a mixture of pity and condescension.

By the time they'd finished eating, it was nearly five p.m. and Takashi didn't want the day to end. 'Can I take you home? I'd like to see your family again. It's not late, and it's been a long time since I've seen your mother.'

'Sure,' she replied.

Takashi felt her hand brush against his arm softly and then pull away quickly. He couldn't tell whether she felt that this was a good idea or not. He was so sure that they'd spent a great day together. There was a definite ease between them, they'd shared a few laughs at lunch and Haruka had been smiling all day. He'd almost felt like her husband as they wandered from here to there, enjoying a day out in Kamakura. Takashi smiled to himself as they both headed back to where the car was parked.

—ᴡᴡ—

It was just before six p.m. when they reached Haruka's house on the corner of a narrow street. Her home was fairly large, yet not in any way pretentious.

'I'm home,' called out Haruka as she opened the door and removed her shoes at the entrance. Takashi could hear her mother coming towards them from the living room.

'Where've you been?' Mrs Yoshino cried out cheerfully. 'We've been waiting for you for over an hour.'

'You knew that I was visiting Kamakura with Takashi today,' Haruka cried back.

Takashi took off his running shoes and carefully placed them to the side at the entrance, next to a very expensive, stylish pair of men's Italian leather shoes that did not look like they would belong to Haruka's father. Doing so, he noticed the hole that he'd forgotten about in his left sock. He pulled at it, trying to move it away from his heel and hide it under his foot.

Mrs Yoshino rushed back to the living room as quickly as she came out of it. Takashi had expected a really big welcome from her, but when she saw him, she only gave him a slight smile and a pert nod, as if they'd only met once before and they were practically strangers. He'd often spoken to Mrs Yoshino when she'd answered his phone calls, and he'd always received a warm welcome in the past when he'd visited her home. Disappointed, Takashi hung his head. He thought afterwards that he must have looked a little like a sulking child as he followed Haruka into their large living room.

Sitting in the Yoshino's plush leather sofa, drinking oolong tea was Yuriko. She was wearing a silver T-shirt and white jeans. She was sitting next to a man a few years older than Takashi that he didn't know. He thought that it was probably the "ex-boyfriend" from Kyoto. Mr Yoshino sat next to them in an armchair, reading the *Yomiuri* newspaper. He glanced up and gave Takashi a pleasant smile and a nod as he entered the room. Although his hair was now white and thinning, he certainly looked a lot healthier than the last time Takashi saw him.

Mrs Yoshino had obviously been entertaining the young people while they were waiting for Haruka.

'Hi Yuriko and Jun, how are you?' asked Haruka.

'Fine, thanks,' said Yuriko and the young man beside her in unison.

'Sorry if you've been waiting for me for a long time. I really wasn't expecting you to drop around until later,' said Haruka.

'Haruka, you look lovely, as usual,' said the young man called Jun with a wide smile.

'Thank you, Jun,' replied Haruka.

'Jun was missing you so much that he insisted we come over earlier,' said Yuriko.

Takashi looked at Jun's face and then over at Haruka's. It killed him to see that Jun was quite smitten with her.

'You know Yuriko Makimoto, my neighbour from next door, and this is Jun Kurokawa, her cousin from Kyoto,' Haruka said to Takashi, looking strangely embarrassed as she beckoned him to take a seat.

'Would you like a glass of chilled barley tea?' Haruka asked Takashi before escaping to the kitchen.

She was out of the room and down the hall before Takashi could reply, leaving him to stare blankly at Yuriko and Jun. Takashi had met Yuriko a few years ago, but he didn't recognise her when he first walked in the room because she'd lost so much weight. He certainly wanted to know how well Haruka knew this Jun guy. He certainly spoke to her like they were boyfriend and girlfriend. Even though he was sitting down, it was obvious that he was taller that six foot. His eyes were as black as midnight and he wore a permanent scowl that lined his deeply tanned face. Jun had an unnatural look about him – his colour was definitely the effect of many hours lying on a sun bed, and when he attempted a smile, Takashi could see that his tombstone teeth had been artificially whitened by the dentist. Takashi wondered why Haruka thought he was attractive. Jun certainly had the arrogance and the look of a player.

Takashi was even more concerned when it became apparent that Mrs Yoshino found Jun captivating. She really seemed to be fascinated by Jun, leaning into him like he was the only person in the room. She sat opposite him and gave him her full attention. Takashi wasn't the jealous type, but he was getting quite wound up watching her dote on Jun's every word. It seemed to Takashi that the attention that he'd once received from Haruka's mother was now being wholly directed at this Jun character.

Takashi tried to look at him now and again, attempting to be inconspicuous. Unfortunately, he did look very cool, dressed in a white T-shirt and navy chino trousers. But Takashi couldn't help noticing that he also had a very annoying habit of running his fingers through his hair every few minutes. He was obviously very conceited.

Unfortunately, Mrs Yoshino seemed to be quite taken by this conceit. Takashi was hurt, but really not so surprised, because next to Jun, he must have looked dishevelled and sweaty from his long day out in the heat.

Haruka finally came back from the kitchen holding a long glass of chilled barley tea. She handed it to Takashi with an apologetic look.

'That's a lovely flower arrangement on the bookcase behind you, Mrs Yoshino,' Jun pointed out.

Takashi hadn't noticed it until now, but he wished that he had and that it was him paying the compliment instead of Jun, who really knew how to charm Haruka's mother. It was upsetting Takashi quite a bit.

'Thank you, Jun,' said Mrs Yoshino. 'Haruka and I take a flower arranging class every Saturday morning.'

'I can see that you're both very talented,' said Jun. 'It's great seeing you all again. I'm only in Ōfune until tomorrow afternoon, and then I have to return to Kyoto. I was telling Yuriko earlier, before we came over, that I was hoping to see you again, Mrs Yoshino. You're originally from Chiba Prefecture, aren't you?'

'Yes, that's right Jun,' she replied. 'And you're from Kyoto of course. Kyoto is such a lovely place.'

'Have you been to Kyoto recently?' Jun asked Mrs Yoshino.

'No, we haven't,' Mrs Yoshino said, staring up at the crooked picture on the opposite wall. 'We visited your parents about three years ago in Kyoto, but my husband and I haven't been back since.'

Mrs Yoshino stood up, leaned over to fluff up a cushion and having done that, walked over to the facing wall and adjusted a picture of a seaside village scene slightly to the left. She stepped back to check and see whether it was level. 'We didn't get to do much sightseeing in Kyoto and I regret that,' Mrs Yoshino continued. She adjusted the picture again a little further to the left, and having done so, came back over to sit down again.

'Well, you should definitely come and visit my family and me in Kyoto again,' Jun suggested. There was a strong conviction in his voice.

Mrs Yoshino's eyes lit up. 'Wouldn't that be wonderful, Haruka!' she said, looking at her daughter.

'Yes, mother,' Haruka replied obediently, but there was excitement written all over her face.

Jun reached for his rucksack and pulled out two presents, beautifully wrapped in distinctive orange boxes.

'Haruka and Mrs Yoshino,' he said. 'I have a couple of small presents for you two lovely ladies.' He handed each of them their gifts, looking at Takashi with a smirk drenched with self-satisfaction.

'More gifts! This is too much,' said Haruka, embarrassed but obviously pleased.

'That's very sweet of you, Jun,' said Mrs Yoshino, opening her present.

The so called "small" presents both turned out to be extremely expensive gifts.

'An Hermès scarf!' both ladies cried out in unison. They opened out their coveted presents, spreading them wide so everyone could appreciate the full effect of each scarf. The rose-coloured luxurious silks were very beautiful. Within minutes, they'd tied their scarves around their necks in fashionable knots.

'How do we look?' asked Mrs Yoshino.

'You both look very stylish. Aren't they nice scarves, Takashi?' Yuriko asked him.

'Oh yes, very stylish,' Takashi stuttered back.

Takashi shifted in his seat and Jun pointed at his foot, having noticed the hole in his sock.

'Takashi, you need to buy yourself a new pair of socks,' he said. Everyone turned to look at the hole in Takashi's sock.

'Yes, you're right, Jun. Well, I have a long trip home. I better get going,' blurted out Takashi, very embarrassed. He finished the last of his barley tea, stood up and walked to the door of the living room. Everyone said his and her goodbyes, but it was only Haruka that showed him to the door.

'I can drive you to the station … wait for me while I get my keys,' she said.

Takashi waited for Haruka in the hallway, listening to the conversation between her mother and Jun in the adjoining room. Jun began telling Mrs Yoshino how he thought her home was lovely and how nice it was to see them again. Hearing this, angry feelings started to well up inside him and he imagined himself rushing in, breaking up this conversation and giving Jun a piece of his mind – but of course, this didn't happen and it wasn't long before Haruka showed up with her keys.

'You know what, Haruka? You must be tired. It's only ten minutes from here to the station, and I'd rather walk.

I'll call you soon. Thanks for today,' Takashi stammered as he made a hasty exit, leaving Haruka, mouth wide open, in the hallway.

Takashi walked down the short driveway and turned to head for the station. He couldn't help but look at the house next door that belonged to Haruka's friend Yuriko as he walked away. He didn't know how he could have ever missed it before. It was a small fortress heavily guarded by huge hedges. Yuriko's family was obviously extremely wealthy and her cousin's family probably had an equally impressive estate. Takashi thought that if there was something going on between Haruka and Jun, she deserved to be with someone who could give her everything. He'd been conceited to think that she could have ever possibly seen him as more than anything but a friend.

On the train heading for home, he did not hear most of the overhead announcements. Takashi was in his own small, unhappy world. He couldn't stop wondering about this Jun he'd met today and how Haruka really felt about him. He thought that the silence during lunch was a bad sign and the whole day had been a series of contradictions. Thinking back, it seemed to him that her words had often been full of encouragement, but at the same time the tone of her voice seemed to discourage him.

Halfway home, having played back over and over in his head the conversations at lunch and at her home between Jun, Haruka and her mother, Takashi started to feel a bit more positive. Surely Haruka preferred him, he thought to himself, and not this pretentious and conceited boy from Kyoto. Although he could not afford to buy Hermès scarves, he decided that he was definitely a better person. With that in mind, he returned to his apartment much happier than when he left Ōfune.

CHAPTER 6

To become wealthy at a single bound

Haruka watched Takashi leave from the entrance of the house. He looked so despondent. *Was it because of the sticky, oppressive weather? Was it because of Jun? Could it have been that they'd spent such a great day together and he hadn't wanted it to end?* She thought to herself.

This was the first time Takashi had met Jun, and Haruka could see how it had unsettled him. After the wonderful day they'd spent together, she'd hoped that he'd realise how much he meant to her as a friend. Haruka was determined not to dwell on this as she went back into the living room. No matter how much she liked Takashi, it was very flattering to receive so much attention from Jun. She paused at the doorway of the room where everyone was seated and watched her mother fawning over Jun with a quiet satisfaction.

Thinking that Jun and the others might be a bit peckish, Haruka decided to replenish her guests' refreshments and without a word, headed into the kitchen, half-listening to the friendly chatter emanating from the living room. She found a packet of rice crackers on the kitchen shelf above the sink. Next, she took out one of her mother's good sculptured wooden bowls from the cupboard above the dishwasher and poured half the packet into it. Haruka reached into the bag to steal a few for herself, wondering whether Yuriko, sitting so happily on the sofa in the next room, would dare to eat even one. Rice crackers were very low in calories, but since Yuriko had developed such an obsession about losing weight over the past few months, she would most probably frown upon placing anything between her lips.

Haruka picked up the bowl, headed back into the living room and sat down next to her mother.

'There you are, Haruka,' said her mother, turning to her. 'Jun was just telling us how his father's real estate company is set to expand overseas next year.'

'Your family's firm really has done very well for itself, hasn't it?' her mother said to Jun. 'Do you think you'll be travelling overseas in the future with your work?' she asked him. Haruka's mother had been dreaming about travel to foreign countries for a long time. Her parents had been to Paris and London many years ago, but it was a short trip, and her mother really would've liked to visit a dozen other countries. As her father's hospital bills had cost them so much, there really wasn't a lot of spare money left to be spent on travel.

'Oh yes,' replied Jun. 'I may even have to live abroad if everything goes as planned.'

Haruka's mother's eyes lit up. The look on her face and the gushing display of enthusiasm she expressed for Jun were evidence that the idea of him as a future son-in-law was once again becoming more and more appealing to her.

Haruka's father leant forward to pick up his glass, and just as quickly her mother jumped to her feet and perched her arm across Yuriko to pass the drink to him.

'Stop fussing over me, woman,' Haruka's father barked at her. His voice was gruff, but his eyes showed both an appreciation and gentle affection for his wife. This made Haruka feel warm and fuzzy inside. In a strange way, her father's illness had brought her parents together, so that they were a lot closer now than before the ordeal.

Haruka shifted her gaze and studied her friend Yuriko as she swayed the conversation in her direction and started babbling on to Jun and Haruka's parents about her shopping experiences in Paris the previous year. Jun nodded attentively while Haruka and her mother watched Yuriko with concern. Her face, covered thickly with makeup, was painfully thin. Her eyes were hollow and her hip bones were jutting out from under her white jeans, giving her body the symmetry of a coat hanger.

Yuriko hadn't touched the rice crackers Haruka had put on the coffee table, although she'd taken a couple of sips from her oolong tea. Haruka knew that her mother would probably comment on Yuriko's appearance as soon as she left the house. Her father wouldn't say anything. He really didn't seem to notice much about people's appearances. Haruka's mother had said once before that she looked ugly and unattractive and that she was behaving like a selfish child. She believed that Yuriko was starving herself just to get attention.

Haruka knew otherwise. Yuriko was far from selfish. She had been slightly overweight in high school and the boys had teased her occasionally. On top of this, her mother hadn't heard the cruel taunts or the bullying some of the more popular girls at school had directed at Yuriko. Haruka remembered the day she'd first spoken to Yuriko. It was Sports Day in her second year at high school and Haruka was heading to the cafeteria for lunch when she noticed Yuriko cowering up against the school gates as three older girls from the year above mocked her for being overweight. She recognised her as the new girl who had just moved into the house next door to her with her family.

Haruka ran up to them and chastised the girls for being mean. The spiteful group by this stage had already said everything they'd wanted to say and it didn't take much for them to leave. From that day on, Haruka had a firm friend and as soon as she and Yuriko realised they both shared a love for Japanese fashion brands, they became inseparable. Many evenings were spent trawling the streets of Ginza, Aoyama and Shibuya looking for outfits to wear on the weekend and to parties. Although Yuriko would sometimes get upset with herself when she couldn't fit into the same clothes as Haruka, that didn't stop the two of them spending most of their free time admiring the latest looks on offer or talking about the current trends.

Yuriko's obsession with her weight developed not long after she returned from Paris. She joined a gym and her weight quickly plummeted. Haruka became concerned that she didn't want to study nor did she want to work. Yuriko spent her days visiting her friends, shopping and exercising and thinking about her boyfriend Ryō. Every time Haruka had visited Yuriko at her home over the past few months, she was either just about to go to or come back from the gym, working out on the exercise bike in her room or on her treadmill in the basement of their huge house.

'Yuriko, why don't you try just one of these rice crackers?' Haruka's mother implored. 'You used to love this type.'

'Oh, no … I need to lose some more weight,' Yuriko replied. 'I'm trying to take off some fat around my calves. Everyone comments on how big my calves are.'

Haruka remembered that Yuriko used to have quite thick calves and ankles, but no one would say that they were large now. She looked across at her mother, who rolled her eyes in Haruka's direction.

'Why don't we go for a walk? It's a little cooler now … Yuriko? Haruka?' said Jun, changing the subject as he stood up and beckoned the others to follow him.

Haruka was just as happy to avoid forcing Yuriko to face her demons and, forgetting she was tired from a long day, she willingly stood up and reached across to help Yuriko up onto her feet. Her mother gently nudged Haruka in the back all the way to the front door.

The weather outside was still nice. Although it had been a lovely day with Takashi, it was very pleasant for Haruka to hear Jun's flattering comments about her dress and her hair as they headed away from the house.

As they turned the corner, Haruka held back a little so she could observe Jun walking slightly ahead with Yuriko. He strutted along like an army major, with a very straight back, as though he was taking charge of the girls. He hadn't always been charming a few years back, but as Haruka looked at him now, all tanned and relaxed, she thought that he'd changed and he was being so nice that it was difficult not to find him attractive.

After about ten minutes, Haruka found it quite difficult keeping up with Yuriko and Jun's pace in this heat. After all, she'd been walking around Kamakura most of the day.

'You'll have to get fitter than that, Haruka, if you want to keep up with us,' teased Jun with a wide grin.

Haruka smiled back at him, not sure how serious he was about this comment. Anyway, she could easily forgive him for being a bit cocky, as he'd given her and her mother such beautiful scarves earlier and they wouldn't have been cheap. The presents really had been very thoughtful, she thought to herself.

Haruka ran up to join them, trying to prove that she was a lot fitter than she actually was, but Jun and Yuriko slowed down for her, sensing how tired she was and she appreciated this as they walked along enjoying the balmy evening.

'I'll be in Kyoto next week for an interview. Jun ... would you like to meet up?'

'What day? I'm quite busy next week with work.'

'Tuesday. My interview is at eleven a.m. ... I'll be finished by midday.'

'Sounds good. I could meet you at twelve p.m. and take you out to lunch.'

'That sounds great.'

'Send me a text message when you've finished the interview,' said Jun.

'I will if you promise to look at your phone – you never answer it when I try and call you.'

'It's just that I'm so busy. I promise I'll check my phone, Haruka.'

'Great,' Haruka said.

They continued walking and Haruka really tried to keep up with Yuriko and Jun, but she was finding this difficult in the stifling humidity, and she really was exhausted after spending the day wandering around Kamakura. Yuriko turned around and must have caught the tired expression on Haruka's face because she pulled at Jun's arm and made him stop walking.

'The cicadas are quite noisy this evening, don't you think?' Yuriko said.

The three of them cocked their heads to listen to the steady chime.

'I think it would be a good idea if we started heading back now. It's too hot and muggy to keep going,' continued Yuriko.

'Good idea,' Jun and Haruka replied simultaneously.

Fifteen minutes later, Haruka returned to her house alone, exhausted and wanting a shower, with thoughts of Jun's charming comments racing through her mind.

Her mother stopped her at the entrance as she was taking off her shoes.

'Have you seen your father's Mont Blanc pen? The one I bought him for his birthday,' she said. 'You know the one, Haruka – the silver and black one with the scratched lid.'

'I saw it on top of the newspaper in the living room this morning before I went out.'

'It's not there now,' said her mother in despair.

Haruka opened the sliding door into the living room. Her father lifted his head above his paper.

'I can't find my new pen,' he announced to her. But without showing any concern, he went back to reading his *Yomiuri* newspaper.

Haruka watched her mother return to the living room and begin turning over cushions. Too tired to help with the search, Haruka hurried out and headed upstairs so that she could be alone. She'd bought two bridal magazines, *Zexy* and *25ans Wedding*, a couple of days before. Sitting on the floor against the bed, she straightened her back, stretched out her legs and started flipping through *Zexy*. She stared at the American couple on the cover. The young girl was looking down at her beautiful bouquet of pink and white roses while her handsome new husband, with his chiselled features, gazed into her eyes with adoration. Both of them looked supremely happy, almost smug, as if this amazing wedding day was just the start of a wonderful future together, with no misgivings or worries. They looked so well-suited and so content. Their smiles gave Haruka the impression that nothing could disturb their perfect lives together.

She thought about her own life and her relationships with Takashi and Jun and how different she'd look standing next to either one of them on her wedding day. Takashi was attractive, very aware of her needs and always very kind; but he was a struggling student who could only promise her a basic lifestyle. She thought that maybe she'd get bored if she married him and start to wish she'd chosen someone who could give her so much more. On the other hand, Jun was extremely wealthy and generous, but egotistical and probably very difficult to live with. Despite these faults, she liked the idea that she could go shopping and buy all her favourite brands if she married him. She could fill her wardrobes with well-cut shirts from Yohji Yamamoto, lovely pleated skirts from Comme des Garçons and lots of handbags from Prada. She'd also be able to indulge her passion for expensive shoes and take trips to Paris and New York with Yuriko whenever she pleased. Haruka bit her lip and smiled to herself. She really enjoyed these images of travel and endless shopping days.

But it didn't take long for her to realise that she hadn't considered the full picture. It soon occurred to her that she wasn't really facing the reality of the situation. Life wasn't an endless shopping trip. Her happiness was paramount, but which one could offer her this happiness – Takashi or Jun?

Haruka had been flicking through the bridal magazines in her bedroom for about two hours, thinking about the pros and cons of marrying Takashi or Jun, when she felt a bit parched and decided to go to the kitchen for some oolong tea. She was walking down the corridor past the living room when she thought she heard her parents talking about Jun. Haruka peeped through the crack in the door and saw her mother kneeling down beside her father, talking quietly. Haruka's father was still sitting in his favourite sofa chair, and even though he still seemed absorbed in the *Yomiuri* newspaper, he was nodding at his wife as she chatted away.

'I think Jun has matured a lot compared to a few years ago,' said her mother. 'He really has turned into a very nice young man.'

'Do you think so?' replied her father.

'Yes, and since he comes from such a good family who are obviously worth a lot of money, we should reconsider him as a future husband for Haruka. I know she likes Takashi, but from what I can gather, he wouldn't be able to really provide for her like Jun could, and did you see the way he was dressed today with that hole in his sock? The more I think about it, the more I know Jun would be a better husband for our daughter.'

'Maybe,' replied Haruka's father.

'You know we've had to be more careful with money since you retired, and as you're no longer an accountant, we can't afford the same lifestyle – and after paying for all your hospital bills … I really don't know what we're going to do in the future. I think we might have to sell the house.'

'Yes, I realise that,' said Haruka's father.

'Couldn't you ask your mother for money, considering she's so wealthy and we've never asked for anything in the past?'

'You know I can't do that,' said her father. 'My mother has never helped us up until now because she believes we should provide for ourselves. Anyway, I'm far too proud to go and ask her for the money. Maybe we should consider meeting with Jun's parents again in Kyoto.'

'That's an excellent idea,' said her mother. 'We should definitely think about going to Kyoto again and we should encourage Haruka to marry Jun and then we would never have to worry about her in the future. We'd know that she was being well looked after and it wouldn't matter if we had no money to pass on to her.'

'Haruka should marry for love, but love where the money is.'

'You're absolutely right.'

'Wait and see how Jun and Haruka are getting along over the next few months and if everything goes well then we should go to Kyoto,' said Haruka's father.

'Yes, I will,' replied her mother.

Haruka quietly pulled herself away from the living room door and tiptoed to the kitchen to get a drink. She was really shaken. It hadn't occurred to her that her parents' money problems were that bad, and she felt guilty for not realising this before now. She had to learn to be a lot more frugal from then on. Her mother was right – Jun would be a better match for her, even though she really liked Takashi. All of a sudden, her fanciful daydreaming earlier on seemed childish and immature.

Haruka decided that no matter how annoying or conceited Jun appeared at times, she'd concentrate on forging a stronger relationship with him to ensure the security of her future. She would make a better effort from then on to like everything about Jun. If she did this, she knew that she'd have to contend with Jun's mother to seal the deal, but she would try her upmost to impress her. Haruka knew that lots of other Japanese girls put on a brave face in front of their in-laws to keep the peace and respect their parents' wishes, and she would try to be as strong as any other girl to win over Jun's mother, Mrs Kurokawa. She told herself that she would rein in her emotions and smile, and be so sweet and courteous that Jun's mother would embrace her and her parents with open arms.

But as the hours passed, the more she thought about it the more she began to doubt herself and she wondered if she could really be the person Mrs Kurokawa wanted her to be. It would be a long time before Haruka fell asleep that night.

CHAPTER 7

Fortune's wheel is ever turning

Haruka received a text message from Yuriko on Monday afternoon at work, asking her to drop in at her house that evening. She said it was of the utmost importance. Haruka was worried that something might be very wrong, as it all seemed very urgent.

At seven thirty p.m., Haruka located her car in the car park at Ōfune station and ten minutes later, she pulled into her driveway at home. Getting out of the car, she stopped for a moment, wondering whether she should take a quick shower before going next door. She was quite hot and a little sweaty. Her white linen dress was crumpled and needed an iron and her cream strappy sandals were digging into her feet a little.

Haruka was hoping Jun had returned to Kyoto, because she didn't want to see him when she wasn't looking her best – but Yuriko's text had sounded pretty urgent and she was just dying to find out what all the fuss was about, so Haruka decided not to freshen up and instead she headed straight over to her house. Yuriko must have been waiting by the entrance, because she opened the front door before Haruka even had a chance to ring the doorbell.

'Come upstairs quickly,' she said to Haruka, tugging at her sleeve. 'I don't want my family to hear what I'm going to tell you.'

The excited look on her face told Haruka that whatever she had to say, it wasn't going to be bad. She followed her up the stairs to her bedroom. As Yuriko led the way, Haruka noticed that she was looking even more gaunt than usual. The white shirt she was wearing only emphasised the bones that were clearly visible on her back and her ribs. In her mind, Haruka cursed Yuriko's two timing ex-boyfriend Ryō, who'd made her feel like she had to be thinner to be more attractive to him.

They reached Yuriko's bedroom and once inside, Yuriko shut the door firmly and started pacing back and forth, wriggling with delight.

'What is it you have to tell me?' Haruka asked, getting caught up in the moment by all the excitement.

'Wait a minute, I just have to check that my younger brother's not listening at the keyhole,' Yuriko whispered. She went to the door, opened it up and looked to the left and the right of the landing. Satisfied that there was no one there, she shut the door again and came back to sit on her candy-striped sofa chair.

'You're not going to believe the news I have to tell you – it's epic!' she said.

'I've been waiting all day. Don't keep me in suspense any longer.'

'Okay Haruka. You really like Jun don't you?'

'Yes.'

'And from what I can tell, he really likes you, doesn't he?'

'Yes.'

'Well, he woke up this morning and told me he was going to Ginza to do some shopping and I said that I'd go with him. However, he absolutely insisted that he go by himself. This, of course, made me wildly curious because he knows I love going into Ginza and it was a bit strange that he wouldn't let me go with him.'

'Yes, I suppose that was a bit strange,' said Haruka, wondering where this conversation was heading.

'So Jun came back from Ginza at about three thirty p.m. and I noticed that he had some shopping bags with him which he left in the living room.'

'Go on,' Haruka said.

'Well, he was planning to return to Kyoto in the next couple of hours and I know it's not the right thing to do, but I had a peek in his shopping bags while he was talking to my mother in the kitchen.'

'That's a bit naughty,' Haruka said, 'but I know what you're like when you see a shopping bag.'

'You're not going to believe what I saw inside the bags,' said Yuriko, pausing for dramatic effect.

'Tell me,' said Haruka, as she leaned forward on the edge of the bed.

'A solitaire diamond engagement ring set in platinum from Wako Department Store!'

'No, you're lying,' said Haruka, nearly falling off the bed.

'No, I'm not, and I bet he bought it to give it to you,' exclaimed Yuriko.

'Do you really think so?' Haruka asked her. 'Tell me what was it like. Was it beautiful – and how big was the diamond?'

'It was the most beautiful engagement ring I've ever seen. It must have been at least two carats and the colour of the diamond looked so radiant to me.'

'Radiant,' echoed Haruka as she drifted into a warm and fuzzy dreamlike state, imagining what the ring might look like.

'You're such a lucky girl, Haruka,' said Yuriko. 'Jun's never really told me how much you mean to him, but I suppose the proof is in the ring he's just bought you.'

'But he returned to Kyoto earlier, didn't he?' Haruka asked her, slowly coming back to reality.

'Yes, maybe he hasn't decided how to ask you to marry him and he needs some time to think about it,' said Yuriko. 'Oh, I bet it will be really romantic. You have to tell me all about it as soon as he pops the question.'

'Of course. You'll be the first person I tell, after my parents,' Haruka said. 'Let's go back to my house and look at the bridal magazines I bought last week. You know what, Yuriko? I don't think we should tell my mother about this yet. Let's keep it our little secret for the moment.'

Yuriko nodded back and they joined their pinkie fingers together and made a promise not to tell anyone.

They rushed out of Yuriko's house and went next door to Haruka's home. As they raced through the door on their way to Haruka's room, her mother stopped them.

'Welcome home Haruka and hello Yuriko,' she said to them, noticing their radiating smiles as they passed. 'What are you two girls up to?' she asked.

'Nothing,' they both cried out in unison.

They went to Haruka's bedroom and flipped through bridal magazines, gossiping and laughing until late. Her room was half the size of Yuriko's bedroom and she had no en suite, but it was cosy enough for them to relax on the floor and keep themselves entertained for the next couple of hours. There were no pink walls or soft toys in Haruka's bedroom, just a bed painted in a neutral shade, a desk for studying, a solid oak wardrobe and matching bedside tables, as well as a pine bookcase lined with a few marketing textbooks and some novels and books dedicated to Japanese history and culture.

Later that night, after Yuriko had left, very pleased with herself for making such a great discovery, Haruka went to bed, but she couldn't sleep. She kept thinking of Takashi and how well they got along, and she almost wished it were him who was about to give her a big diamond engagement ring. She even shed a few tears thinking about how much she'd miss their Thursday night evenings at the café and the easy-going conversations that they'd always shared.

After she'd been sobbing for about ten minutes, Haruka recalled her father's words: "marry for love but love where the money is..." Thinking about this, she told herself she was being silly and a hopeless romantic. She couldn't live on rice alone, and Jun would be able to provide her with all the lovely material things that she'd wanted in life and she'd never want for anything again. Haruka told herself that Jun was a much more mature and practical choice, and above everything else, by marrying Jun, she was going to keep her dear parents happy. Haruka was really looking forward to meeting Jun for lunch when she went to Kyoto for her interview the following week. Her mind whirled with images of that diamond ring and wedding plans. It wasn't until about three a.m. that she finally drifted off to sleep.

CHAPTER 8

Other times, other manners

Haruka had chosen a navy pinstripe suit, a cream silk
shirt and a comfortable yet smart pair of three-inch black
heels to wear to her interview in Kyoto. She had to be
there for eleven a.m. and because the bullet train was
leaving just after eight a.m. from Shin-Yokohama station,
there'd been a mad rush in the morning to get to the
station on time.

Luckily, there were no delays and she boarded the nine
past eight high-speed Nozomi bullet train on platform
four with a few minutes to spare before it left
the station. Haruka tried to spend the time on board
reading up on the requirements of the management
position, but her mind kept switching back to thoughts of
engagement rings and wedding parties. She sent Jun a
text message telling him that she was on her way to
Kyoto, as well as where to find her at the English
conversation school, and she confirmed she could meet
him for lunch at twelve p.m. He replied to her text almost
immediately, telling her that he was looking forward to
meeting up with her. Haruka's heart skipped a beat; this
was all becoming very exciting. She kind of hoped there
might be some talk about wedding plans or engagement
rings at lunch. It did occur to her that it would be

unrealistic for her to receive a proposal over a quick lunch, but the mere thought of it made her feel like liquid gold was running through her veins.

After a two-hour journey, Haruka exited Kyoto station and caught a taxi to the English conversation school that was centrally located in the middle of town. Less than ten minutes later, she found herself standing in front of the school building. She'd been told that administration was on the third floor and all the teaching was conducted on the fourth floor. She was to report to the third floor and ask for Mrs Aoki.

After checking that her makeup hadn't spoiled in the heat, she stepped into the elevator. It was only a couple of minutes before she reached the main reception and introduced herself to the young girl at the front desk. It was exactly ten fifty a.m. and the whole floor was buzzing with staff, foreign teachers and students. It could easily have been Haruka's school back in Tokyo, except for the fact that you could occasionally hear a snippet of the Kansai dialect representing this side of the country.

Five minutes later, Mrs Aoki introduced herself to Haruka and led her to a cubicle set aside from the reception area. She was a very tall and thin lady, dressed in a black mid-length linen shift dress, and she had a beautiful necklace strung with fine cultured pearls around her neck that matched her earrings. She was very officious, yet friendly with Haruka, but the rest of the staff seemed a little bit terrified of her.

'You're Haruka Yoshino,' Mrs Aoki said. 'Am I right?'

'Yes, I am,' Haruka replied. 'I've just come from Tokyo to apply for the manager's position.'

'Yes, very good,' she said. They sat down and Mrs Aoki took out a pen and started making notes on the papers in front of her.

'This is a very important position, and it requires you to work hard. You need to gain the respect of the other staff members and be able to communicate well with the foreign teachers without any conflict,' Mrs Aoki said to Haruka without looking up, scribbling notes at the same time. 'You've been chosen for this position because of your capabilities and experience. The woman who has been doing this job up until now has had an excellent understanding of the role; it's just a pity she's planning to move to the US to live with her boyfriend.'

'The role requires you to take charge of three of our girls in administration. You'll also need to organise the timetables for all our foreign teachers, and they'll come to you if they have any problems,' said Mrs Aoki, looking Haruka straight in the eye. 'You will have a meeting once a month with the other two administration managers and a separate meeting with me in which I shall track your progress.' Mrs Aoki referred to her notes and continued, 'We'd like you to start in the third week of February and we expect you to move into the accommodation we'll have organised for you in the previous week ... has your manager in Tokyo talked to you about the salary?'

'Yes, thank you,' Haruka replied. 'That's absolutely fine.' In fact, Haruka thought it was a lot better than fine.

'Your manager tells me that your English is quite good – however, we expect all our staff here to speak excellent English, so I presume you'll continue with your lessons here on a weekly basis?'

'I certainly will.'

'I have some forms for you to complete,' Mrs Aoki said. 'I'll be back in a moment.'

Mrs Aoki left the cubicle and Haruka waited about fifteen minutes for her to return. She could hear her voice now and then asking various staff members to do this or that.

A quarter of an hour later, Mrs Aoki returned to the cubicle and passed Haruka an envelope, but she didn't sit down.

'I need you to complete these forms and post them back to me by November.'

Haruka accepted the envelope with her name on it.

'You also need to complete a one week training course at our school in Nihombashi in the first week of February,' Mrs Aoki said to Haruka. 'Is that clear?'

'Yes, it is.'

'Good. I have a very busy day, so I must finish up now … here is my business card.'

Mrs Aoki passed this to Haruka. She accepted it with both hands and a respectful nod.

'Feel free to call me at any time if you have any questions before you start in February – and of course, you can make an appointment at any time to see me if you're in Kyoto.' With that, Mrs Aoki picked up her notes, pushed her chair back under the desk and stepped to the side. 'Thank you for coming today, Haruka – it was very nice to meet you.'

'It was very nice to meet you, too,' Haruka replied. 'Thank you for your time.'

Haruka walked quickly back to the elevator, but just before its door opened, she turned her head and looked back to see Mrs Aoki summoning three girls into her office for another meeting. Haruka was relieved that her interview was over and she'd secured the management position.

Haruka stepped out of the building flushed and quite drained. It was eleven thirty a.m. and she had thirty minutes before she was supposed to meet with Jun. She took out the envelope that Mrs Aoki had given her with the intention of going over the requirements for her new role. Her eyes were on the paper, but she saw Jun's face on the page, rather than the Japanese characters. About fifteen minutes later, Haruka received a tap on the shoulder. She turned to see Jun smiling down at her.

'You're early,' Haruka exclaimed, jumping back in surprise. She looked him up and down and thought he looked very smart in his grey suit, white shirt and mauve silk tie. *Maybe he has a ring in his pocket?* she thought to herself.

'I was looking forward to seeing you,' he replied. 'Would you like to eat sushi? I know this place not far from here that does decent conveyer belt sushi.'

'Sounds good,' Haruka said, beaming from ear to ear.

Jun led Haruka away from town down various narrow streets until they arrived at his chosen eatery. It was quite crowded inside, and they had to wait ten minutes for a seat.

'How was your interview?' Jun asked Haruka.

'I think it went well. I start in February.'

'Good,' replied Jun without much enthusiasm.

Haruka thought he would've been happier for her, but she told herself he probably wanted her to give up work once they were married, and thinking that cheered her up.

'What time is your train leaving for Tokyo?' Jun asked Haruka.

'One thirty p.m.,' she replied, just as two seats became available and they were invited to sit down.

Within seconds, Jun had started taking dishes off the conveyer belt for both of them. By the end of the meal, he'd finished off seven plates and Haruka had eaten five. It all seemed a bit rushed, and he was more intent on eating rather than making conversation.

'What's the hurry?' Haruka asked.

'I should really be at work ... my father thinks I'm viewing a new property right now that has just come on to the market, and he'll be expecting me back at the office soon.'

'I don't want you to get into any trouble,' Haruka said half-heartedly. 'Maybe I should go to the train station now and let you get back to work.' She really expected him to turn around, apologise and tell her that he'd much rather spend time with her than make his way back to the office, but he didn't.

'Yes, Haruka, I should really get back to the office,' he said as he paid for the meal and led her out into the street. 'But I'll hail a taxi and accompany you to the train station.'

'I'd much rather walk,' Haruka replied.

'No, it would be much quicker by taxi,' said Jun, raising his hand in the air and with that a taxi pulled up right in front of them. The back door opened automatically and he nudged Haruka in, following her close behind.

Haruka didn't know why they needed to get a taxi. It only took five minutes to get to the station. Once there,

Jun leaned forward and asked the driver to wait a moment while he said goodbye to her – but he had no plans to wait inside the station with Haruka, although her train didn't leave for another fifty minutes. He simply waved to her as the back door of the taxi closed and the car pulled away. He'd left in a sea of traffic before she could even say a proper goodbye.

Haruka waited for her train inside the station, feeling a bit upset and confused. The lunch had not gone as well as she expected, and she wondered whether she'd been rude to Jun without realising it. She went over and over the lunch scene in her mind all the way back on the train. Her relationship with Jun didn't seem right to her, and her mind was in turmoil trying to work out what was wrong. She arrived back in Tokyo feeling wretched, worn out and perplexed.

CHAPTER 9

*Even a chance acquaintance
is decreed by destiny*

Takashi continued with his studies throughout the summer. The long, hot and humid days finally ended, and October began. Cooler breezes swept through the city like gentle kisses. Over the past few months, he had been disappointed that so many of his Thursday night meetings with Haruka had been cancelled. She'd tell him she had to work late or her mother was expecting her home early for one reason or another. When they did get to meet, she didn't seem as friendly. If anything, she seemed distracted, and Takashi was worried that their friendship was beginning to unravel. Their regular phone calls had also been reduced to once a week and this left a gnawing ache in his stomach.

From Monday to Saturday, Takashi's daily routine would centre on his studies at home. This was only broken up by an important lecture at university that he felt compelled to attend. If he thought that the lecture would have no significance in relation to his exams, he would not show up. He would ask a friend for the notes and use this time to his advantage and study at home.

Takashi was basically living off ready meals from the convenience store. For lunch, he would usually buy a fried ham sandwich for just ¥210. He was also partial to the dumpling set, although they weren't as nice as the ones that he could buy at the station. Most evenings at about seven or eight p.m., Takashi would walk to the convenience store between his apartment and the station and choose between a small sushi pack or fried rice and cold Zaru soba noodles. The previous winter when the weather had been cooler and if he'd had enough money, he'd often buy croquettes on rice or his favourite dish, lemon and spicy chicken with rice.

Takashi could either get the convenience store to heat his food up or just zap it in the microwave back at his place. He made it a rule to only eat at MOS Burger once a month, because he was always tempted to eat more than he should. Takashi had never been a great cook – probably due to the fact that his mother was significantly better than other mothers in the kitchen. This room had always been his mother's domain and to enter into it and to try and experiment would have been sacrilegious. It would have been equal to a waiter attempting to make the Special of The Day in a restaurant renowned for having a famous chef.

On Sundays, Takashi would meet Masaya for some time-out, but on every other day of the week, he would most often hibernate in his apartment with his head lost in his textbooks. If anyone were to come and visit him, they'd probably have thought something was wrong. Sometimes he didn't shower or shave for days at a time. If he'd bought enough food from the store the week before, he wouldn't have to go to the convenience store and he could stay at his place and study in his old sweats all day every day.

Takashi tried very hard to be disciplined and sensible, but he would sometimes procrastinate and put off his studies until the next day. When he spoke to his mother, she would often tell him that he should try and be more mature and it was time for him to grow up. He wanted to please her and be like this, but he loved the company of his friends. He especially valued the time he spent with

Masaya, and most Sundays he would close his books, smarten himself up and go on long walks with him to clear his head and prepare himself for the week ahead.

He often thought about his relationship with Haruka, and he kept trying to think of ways that he could make it better, but he was afraid that she was now spending more time with Jun and she was also very busy at work. Takashi understood that she was very committed to her job, and when she phoned him with excuses, saying she couldn't meet up for one of their dates, he'd tell her not to worry because he was busy with his studies. This wasn't entirely true, but he didn't want her to feel bad.

The devil inside him made him wonder if she was getting bored meeting up with him. When Takashi called her at home earlier that week, her mother told him that Jun had been over to visit her again, and this worried him. He presumed the worst and again he wondered if she was no longer interested in him. Despite this, Takashi continued to send her text messages, not ready to give up on her yet.

Takashi also spoke to his high-school chum Kenji whenever he had a chance, but he never really had the time to meet with him. Kenji was always working in Ginza or out on a date with a different girl. Takashi lost track of who he was actually seeing.

On Sundays, his long walks became his way of diffusing the tension that his studies created. Takashi found that walking through the department stores and looking in the shop windows helped him to relax. His adventures also helped him, whether he was consciously aware of it or not, to take in trends in branding, advertising and new marketing concepts. The shops that Takashi and his friends liked recognised the need to constantly reinvent new ways to keep them coming back to their stores. With consumers in Japan becoming more and more frustrated with companies bombarding them with constant advertising, the more savvy retailers realised they had to think about introducing subtle marketing techniques and look beyond handing out free tissues at the train stations with their logo on the front.

These days out also made Takashi feel part of the human race. All that study in his cramped and smoky apartment could easily take its toll on him. Takashi's walks with Masaya also gave him the opportunity to get some solid exercise and on the train there and back home again he could review what he had done over the past week and this helped him to decide what he would do with the next few days ahead of him.

It was the second Sunday in October when Takashi set out from his apartment with a view to visiting Shibuya and Daikanyama with Masaya. These were two of their favourite haunts. He was dressed in faded denim jeans and a black cotton sweater. His camel-coloured lumberjack boots finished off the look.

Takashi walked to Kawasaki station. His eyes followed the usual path that he always walked – a straight road bordered by shops and the occasional restaurant. Rows and rows of bikes were lined up against the footpath, waiting for their owners to finish their shopping or return after having spent the last of their change gambling in the Pachinko parlours. He had a lot on his mind. He was going over and over some statistical models that he'd studied the night before.

It was only about two hundred metres from the station when Takashi suddenly realised that the ground was covered in amber and golden caramel leaves. It was like someone had come down in the middle of the night and used the rain to glue a mosaic leaf formation all over the paths for the enjoyment of the pedestrians. He smiled; knowing that autumn had well and truly arrived and those long, humid nights were finished for yet another year. He now walked with more purpose in his step, and he looked forward to the months ahead.

Takashi boarded the train on the Tokkaido line to get to Shinagawa and from there, took the Yamanote line to Shibuya. Exiting the train, he had to weave through a swarm of people to reach the main exit. Masaya was waiting next to the bronze Hachiko dog statue, dressed in a pair of Levi's and a blue and white long-sleeved top.

'Hey, I've been here for fifteen minutes. Did you miss your train?' he teased Takashi.

'I was daydreaming on the way to the station.'

He poked Takashi in the arm. 'Daydreaming about Haruka?'

'No,' Takashi said, blushing.

'Aah,' screamed Masaya, laughing at Takashi's embarrassment. 'C'mon, let's go. I want to buy some house slippers from Loft.'

The central scramble crossing was ahead of them and when the lights turned green, they joined the hundreds of people crossing diagonally in eight directions to reach the shops and the department stores on the opposite side.

As usual, Shibuya was a beehive of twenty-something adults and young and hip adolescents. The area breathed a spirit of enthusiasm and youth. Neon signs beamed down on hundreds of shoppers weaving like a colony of ants – but a very fashionable colony. If you were perched at the tops of the buildings, you'd look down to see a wave of beings out to impress. Long hair down to the waist, shaved heads showing off intricate tattoos; fashionable hats and hairpieces and all other styles of headwear adorned the thousands of fashionistas out to impress each other.

Hundreds of shopping bags were held by their bearers as symbols of style and sophistication. A proportion of them were standing alone on corners waiting for friends, their eyes flicking over passers-by with approval or disapproval. Groups of three of four girls could be seen here and there expertly navigating their way through the crowds as one as they were nudged through this sea of consumerism. Slightly older singletons headed determinedly towards their chosen department store or boutique, their set and confident expressions showing others they were experts in the art of shopping and knew the area better than most.

Takashi and Masaya passed the HMV music shop to reach Loft, one of their favourite interior design and gift complexes. They liked to walk through each of its seven floors, and although he didn't often buy anything, Takashi always liked to see what he'd purchase if he had more money. He liked to imagine the type of living space he'd create and how great it would look filled with bits and pieces he could buy at Loft and the other trendy stores.

They entered the store and stopped at the sunglasses counter on the first floor.

'Go on, try these,' Masaya said, holding up a pair of tortoiseshell glasses for Takashi to try on.

Takashi checked the price before putting them on with some hesitation and peered into the mirror on the counter.

'I'm not sure about these Masaya,' Takashi said. 'They're very expensive.'

Masaya came over and stood facing Takashi, turning his head from one side to the other to inspect him.

'They look terrific on you,' he said.

Takashi put the glasses back onto the rack and left Masaya to try on several other pairs. A couple of minutes later bored with that, he wandered over to the wristwatch section. He was enjoying this leisurely afternoon and Masaya seemed to be having fun too.

Masaya came over and pointed towards the escalator. 'We have to go up to level five. Don't you remember that I wanted to get some house slippers?'

'Oh yeah,' Takashi replied.

Masaya waved the floor guide at him. 'Did you know that Momo-chan is going to move in with me soon?' he asked Takashi when they reached the escalator.

Takashi gave him a friendly punch. 'Does that mean you're going to get married?'

'No way! Me – married? I don't think so. No, she can keep the place clean,' said Masaya, laughing cheekily.

'I thought she had her own apartment.'

'Yes, she did,' said Masaya. 'She started renting a place when she began working for a diamond company in Shinjuku. She had to keep working there to pay the rent, but her boss was really shady and he was giving her a hard time. I went to meet her after work a couple of weeks ago and after meeting her boss, I told her to quit and move in with me,' explained Masaya.

'The poor girl.'

'I know. That job was becoming really stressful for her, but she'll be alright now.'

'Thanks to you, Masaya.'

'Well, people say I'm a great guy,' said Masaya. He burst into laughter, turning his back on Takashi just before they reached the fifth floor. Five seconds later, they approached the racks of slippers they'd been looking for. Masaya picked up a tan pair and then reached for another pair in the same colour and style, but in a smaller size.

'I'll take these. ¥1,000 each! Not a bad price,' he said turning the two pairs over in his hands to feel their texture. 'Made in France! Cool!'

'Do you need anything else?' Takashi asked.

'Let's go and look at the clothes in Seibu department store next door.'

'No problem,' Takashi said with a smile.

They crossed the road and entered the Seibu store.

'Do you remember what floor the men's wear is on?' asked Masaya, pointing to the upper floors.

'Fourth floor,' Takashi replied firmly.

They reached the fourth floor and checked out the labels that were on display: Giorgio Armani, Comme des Garçons Edited, Yohji Yamamoto, Joseph Homme, Porsche Design, Ralph Lauren Black Label and many others. They wandered through these boutiques quite quickly, trying not to attract too much attention from the shop assistants.

Having checked out the fashions upstairs, they headed back to the escalator. A tall man in a black tuxedo stood politely to the side of the down escalator, offering a glass of Moët Champagne to shoppers.

Masaya and Takashi looked at each other and silently agreed to take a glass.

'There we are,' the gentleman in black said, handing both of them a quarter filled glass. 'Are you looking for a particular designer?' he asked.

The man in black did speak very beautifully.

'Ah. Um. Ah,' Takashi stuttered.

'We're here to view the latest Armani collection for the season,' said Masaya confidently, in a very posh voice.

'Very good,' replied the gentleman in black.

Masaya and Takashi quickly quaffed the rest of the Champagne and rushed down the escalators to the exit. Outside, they bent over backwards with laughter.

Takashi stood stiffly upright and mimicked Masaya with an over-affected posh voice. 'We're here to view the Armani collection!'

'Shut up,' said Masaya. 'Ah, um, ee, um!' he mimicked him. 'Come on, Takashi, let's go to Daikanyama.'

'Okay,' Takashi agreed. 'But let's get something to eat first. It's cheaper to eat in Shibuya.'

'Sure,' said Masaya.

They ended up walking through a few more shops, all packed tightly together in this pulsating shopping district, before finding somewhere to eat.

Many of the shop windows were cleverly designed to lure customers through their doors. Takashi tried not to become a victim to many of these tempting invitations. Having been here so many times before, he rarely parted with a lot of money, strongly aware that he had to live on a tight budget while he was at university. *When I start working in marketing,* he kept telling himself, *I shall eventually have enough money to buy whatever my heart desires.*

It had been three hours since Takashi had left his apartment. His feet were tired and his stomach was groaning. They finally found a cheap little vendor where, for a few hundred yen, they were able to buy chicken and rice dishes. They had to stand and eat against a counter. This place was cramped between a department store and a small music shop and although it was a small eatery, it was very popular. They stood there surrounded by couples and young men who were shopping solo. The food and the customers were churned out quickly, and it wasn't long before they were finished. Feeling a lot better, they went on their way again.

They decided to visit the Kinokuniya bookshop opposite the station before making their way to

Daikanyama. They moved through the crowded store like a tight school of fish, shoulder to shoulder with dozens of other strangers, each of them searching for their chosen novel or magazine. When they reached the section on comic books, it was too crowded for Takashi to steal a good look at the latest choices. They left after only a few minutes, excusing themselves over and over again as they pushed their way through the crowds and back down the escalator. Finally, they reached the ground floor and from there they made their way to the train station.

Takashi always enjoyed visiting Daikanyama after window-shopping in Shibuya. There was a great deal less hustle and bustle in this town. It was only the affluent that could afford to live in this area, and there was a possibility of running into arrogant shoppers and sales assistants, but Takashi really found it all very sophisticated.

After taking the Tōkyū Tōyoko line from Shibuya, they arrived in Daikanyama. They wandered through the streets leading from the station, which were more like lanes or winding paths compared to the noisy and bustling stretches of bitumen that ran through Shibuya. They stopped to admire a red Ferrari parked on the side of the road. You could see the whole engine under its transparent cover. Takashi thought that it really would have been so cool to be able to walk up to it and claim this car as their own, put the key in the door, sit in the red leather bucket seats and wrap their fingers around the stitched leather steering wheel with its yellow Ferrari emblem. The owner of this car certainly wasn't a university student with a limited income. He was probably a music producer or an owner of one of the boutiques or restaurants nearby, Takashi thought to himself.

The streets were lined here and there with the occasional stylish boutique, some of which they popped into to take a look at the latest clothes. There were also classy cafés and society restaurants on every corner. Takashi sometimes made plans before their visit to work up the courage to try on the markedly expensive clothes, hoping to be attended by a gorgeous-looking sales assistant, but he just couldn't bring himself to do it. Their friend Kenji would've been able to do it with ease, while at the same time laughing his way through it. At the end of it all, he would have no trouble completely convincing the ladies in the shop that he would be back later to pick the clothes up. He'd probably get a date out of it too, somehow.

Feeling a little tired now after wandering through these exclusive shops, looking but of course not trying on the clothes, they settled on getting a coffee from one of the cafés near the train station. They were hoping to sit in their courtyard for a while and rest a little before heading back home.

It wasn't until Takashi bought his coffee at the counter of their chosen café from a girl with a piercing through her chin, complemented by several more on her eyebrows, that he realised there were not that many places to sit down.

Suddenly, a familiar voice called out his name, sounding very much like Haruka. Takashi's face lit up to see her sitting, as composed as ever, on a leather sofa in the back corner. She was waving her hand from left to right in the elegant way that only beautiful girls knew how. He rushed towards her and nearly knocked his coffee over a huge foreign man.

'*Whhhooooo ... careful!*' cried out the large man in English in a big voice.

Takashi had slowed down anyway at this point, because he'd just spotted Jun and Yuriko, sitting to Haruka's right. He silently winced, noticing Jun's left arm casually resting on Haruka's shoulders.

Takashi excused himself as everyone edged further over to the right and he sat down on Haruka's left. It was a snug fit, but he was as happy as anything to be the cushion squeezed between the wall and this lovely girl, and even happier that Jun had now taken his arm off Haruka's shoulder.

Takashi introduced Masaya to Yuriko and Jun, and he sat facing everyone in the seat opposite, looking at

Takashi, then Jun and then back at Takashi again, while Haruka apologised for being unable to meet Takashi on Thursday. When she fell silent, there was a long pause, and for a second, they all looked very uncomfortable before Yuriko piped up with a recount of the day that Jun, Haruka and she had shared so far.

Takashi looked across the table, still a bit hungry after his lunch in Shibuya. Haruka was enjoying a French hot dog in a baguette with a salad on the side. Yuriko was playing with her Caesar salad and Jun looked like he'd finished his lunch. While Haruka ate her lunch, he tried to draw her attention in, chatting away about the different shops and the Champagne that the department store was serving in Shibuya.

'It's a great idea, Haruka,' said Takashi. 'If I'd had a load of money on me and they kept offering me another glass of bubbly, I know I'd just continue buying clothes and get completely drunk in the process.'

Jun interrupted. 'You're talking about shopping at Seibu … I bought a pair of jeans there last month. They cost me nearly ¥40,000, but no one offered me Champagne,' he said to them as he ran his fingers over and through his hair.

Yuriko ignored Jun. 'I know what you're saying, Takashi. I went into a shop in Aoyama the other day and they were offering a free cup of tea and a piece a cake at the café next to the shop if a customer spent over ¥10,000.'

Jun pushed his way into the conversation once again, 'Oh yes, I know that shop. I was with you when we saw the sign.'

This time Haruka turned to Jun and smiled. 'That's right, Jun – it was last Friday, wasn't it?'

Takashi started to wonder if it was possible for Jun to let other people talk without his continual interruption and why Haruka had never noticed this annoying fact. Although the girls didn't seem to find him aggravating and overly self-assured, Takashi certainly did.

Eventually, Takashi gave up continually trying to vie for Haruka's attention, fearing that he may be mirroring

Jun's maddening habits. Instead, Takashi began to surreptitiously study Yuriko, who was almost a watered down version of her cousin – not so exasperating, but certainly not as pleasing to the eye or the ear as Haruka. From where he was sitting, he could see that Yuriko wore too much make-up for a girl her age, and probably had quite a severe acne problem under all that muck. She was also too lanky for the clothes she was wearing, although they were obviously expensive. He could see the brand Moschino on her top, Chloe on her handbag and Salvatore Ferragamo on her shoes.

After seeing Yuriko's house next door to Haruka's, Takashi knew that she was not the type that would have to resort to any fake brands. Haruka once told him that she never wore more than one label showing at a time – she'd told him that it could look overdone. Looking at her friend now, Takashi thought that Yuriko could do with some of that advice.

He returned his gaze to Haruka. It was easy to appreciate her fine features and charming personality. For this reason, he couldn't understand how someone as nice and intelligent as her would have allowed someone like Jun to rest his arm on her shoulders. Many people had told Takashi that he was a sensible person and that he was able to judge most situations wisely. With those words in mind, he refused to believe that Haruka was seriously interested in Jun, despite the fact he kept popping up all over the place.

Takashi decided that he needed to get Haruka alone. He needed to find out what kind of feelings she had for him and more importantly, whether she could ever see him as more than just a friend. However, on a Sunday afternoon in the middle of a busy café, surrounded by everyone, Takashi knew he wasn't going to find out anything about her true feelings that day.

Masaya and Takashi continued to talk about shops and Shibuya and a new French restaurant that had just opened in Daikanyama where Yuriko had already dined. When Haruka began talking, Takashi nodded away, listening along while he admired her pretty face. Her hair was pulled back into a casual knot that the girls called a chignon, and she was wearing a flowing cream silk jacket and trousers that matched her flat brown shoes. Haruka always wore minimal make-up, and today was no exception. She looked so stylish, and Takashi was so proud to sit next to her. Haruka paused for a moment, and Jun leaned over to question her.

'Would you like to go out for dinner next Thursday night, Haruka? I know this exquisite restaurant in Ginza that serves formal kaiseki ryōri.'

'Oh that would be lovely, Jun,' Haruka enthusiastically responded, to Takashi's dismay, 'but I usually meet Takashi on a Thursday, so couldn't we make it another night?'

'Impossible,' Jun replied. 'I'm going back to Kyoto tomorrow morning and then I'll only be back for twenty-four hours on Thursday, so it can't be any other day.'

'I see,' said Haruka. 'You don't mind if I go out with Jun instead of meeting at our usual café on Thursday, do you Takashi?'

'No, Haruka, that's fine,' Takashi replied, noting how happy Haruka looked. She'd turned her shoulders towards Jun and she was leaning into him. Takashi felt ignored, and he was doing his very best not to show how much this upset him.

'Well, that's settled. Now what are we going to do tonight?' asked Jun. 'Takashi has to study, but I could take you girls out to a club or a nice restaurant in Ōfune or Kamakura. Name your favourite place,' said Jun with a big grin. Again, he was unable to resist the temptation to flick his hair. 'Would you like to join us, Masaya?'

'No, thanks, I have some work to do at the tavern,' Masaya replied.

'Let's go out another night, it's been a long day,' said Yuriko.

Takashi's head started buzzing. It was time for him to leave.

'We have to go. I'll call you in a couple of days, Haruka. Bye everyone,' he said. Masaya and Takashi stood up and walked away. Just near the door, Takashi cursed as he fell over three chairs in his rush to get out of the café.

At Daikanyama station, Masaya and Takashi intended to part ways. Masaya wanted to visit a friend who lived nearby before returning to his tavern. Just before Takashi started to run for his train, Masaya pulled a Loft bag out of his backpack and threw it at him.

'What's this?' Takashi yelled at him.

'A present for my best mate,' he yelled back.

Surprisingly for five p.m., there weren't too many people on the train and Takashi found a seat easily. He opened the Loft bag to find a smallish box inside. Takashi opened it and discovered the sunglasses that Masaya had made him try on in the department store. Any feelings of discontent that he was harbouring from that afternoon after leaving the café now vanished, thanks to his generous friend.

CHAPTER 10

One of these days is none of these days

On Wednesday night, Haruka was bubbling with excitement, wanting to tell everyone about her date the following evening, and she did exactly what she'd promised Yuriko she would not do.

Haruka was at home on her way to the kitchen to get some snacks at about eight p.m. when she saw her mother at the dining table going over the bills and the weekly shopping list. She was slumped in the chair with her head in her hands, and Haruka just felt so sorry for her. Her parents didn't know that she'd heard them discuss their financial problems a few weeks back, and it tore her apart to watch them try and put on a happy, united front for her sake. She'd been playing along as if nothing was wrong so as not to wound her parents' pride, but watching her mother sitting down so depressed at the table, she thought her news about Jun was just what she needed to hear.

Haruka came over and, much to her mother's surprise, knelt beside her and explained how Yuriko had seen the engagement ring and where Jun hoped to take her to dinner the following evening. The result was instantaneous. Her mother broke into a wide smile and clapped her hands. Haruka apologised for not telling her sooner and she told her not to worry. She left the room so pleased that her relationship with Jun had brought so much joy to her mother. The mood in the house changed for the better that night, and Haruka felt a real attachment to her parents that she had not experienced before.

On Sunday, when Jun had asked Haruka out to dinner, both she and Yuriko had shared a knowing smile. Haruka wished Takashi hadn't been there to see her reaction, but at least he didn't know how important that invitation was for her. Yuriko and Haruka had spent most of the week talking about what would happen in Ginza during the date on Thursday.

All week, after Yuriko had spotted the engagement ring in Jun's shopping bag, they'd talked about the special dinner that Jun had arranged. They'd decided that men didn't take you out for kaiseki-ryōri unless it was an important occasion, and for three days they'd only talked about what Haruka would wear that evening, how Jun would propose and how Haruka would react when he popped the question.

It had been decided after several deliberations that Haruka would wear her black lace dress, fitted grey peplum jacket and the Christian Louboutin shoes with the red soles and five-inch heels that she'd bought twelve months before. Jun told Haruka that he was going to meet her at six p.m. outside the English conversation school where she worked in Harajuku, and from there they would go to the restaurant in Ginza.

Since Monday, Haruka had wanted to share her good fortune with the other girls at work, but she'd decided not to tell them because she knew if she waited, a beautiful diamond engagement ring would sum up everything she was dying to say.

On Thursday after work, quite a few girls did ask questions when Haruka changed out of her work clothes and into the black lace dress, but she just smiled and told them she was meeting a friend for a nice dinner in Ginza.

Haruka was outside her workplace at five forty-five p.m. waiting for Jun. It was quite difficult to stand in one place in such high heels, but she gathered inner strength and poise knowing that these beautiful shoes were worth any discomfort if they impressed Jun even a little. He sauntered up to her at about six fifteen p.m. wearing cream chino trousers and a nice, but quite casual, blue striped shirt. It disappointed her a little that he hadn't made a bigger effort, but the fact that he only would have brought an overnight bag from Kyoto justified his looking so casual.

Jun gave Haruka a peck on her cheek in front of some of her colleagues as they were coming out of the school, and she blushed with the pleasure of them seeing her with such a tall and striking man. He led the way to Harajuku train station, and they sat in silence on the train to Ginza.

At the restaurant, the food was served by a young girl in a very attractive kimono. Jun commented on how lovely she looked and Haruka wished she'd dressed in one of the many kimonos that she owned. She consoled herself with the fact that it would have been impossible, as they'd met after work – and anyway, she thought her black dress was equally flattering.

The sweet wine aperitif and the hot sake that they kept drinking throughout the course of the meal helped quieten the butterflies in Haruka's stomach. Her expectations for that night meant that she was unable to eat a lot of the exquisite dishes set out before her, as she kept waiting for the moment when Jun would ask her to marry him. She'd worked out that it wouldn't be very difficult for him to be romantic and go down on one knee, as they were already sitting on the tatami flooring.

They talked about the weather, Tokyo life compared to Kyoto life, her English conversation lessons and her plans to take up the management position in Kyoto, but at no point did Jun lead towards a proposal. Haruka even tried to steer the conversation in the direction of how important it was to find a good husband and how she'd like to have children before she was thirty, but her words fell on deaf ears and Jun kept changing the conversation to talk about his work or something irrelevant such as the cars he'd like to buy.

Haruka enjoyed the meal, but it finished without any indication that he was going to pop the question, and the hot sake was now making her feel flustered and annoyed. They left the restaurant at just eight p.m. Jun asked Haruka if anything was wrong as they headed to the train station to return home, but it would have been presumptuous of her to ask why he hadn't proposed. The moments that he could have used to ask the most important question in her life were now lost.

Tears welled up at the back of her eyes as she sat next to him on the train back to Ōfune and she fought to regain her composure. She didn't want Jun to discover her real reason for being emotional on the long train journey. Her mother would be waiting to hear about wedding plans as soon as she walked in the door, and all she'd be able to talk to her about was what she had for dinner. She told Jun she was just really tired and they sat in silence while she wondered whether she should avoid the subject about weddings altogether or be completely honest with her mother and Yuriko when she saw them next. They both knew her so well that they'd know how disappointed she was with the way everything was working out. Haruka tried to feel better with the consolation that she hadn't said anything to her work colleagues about the proposal.

Obviously, men do take women out for traditional kaiseki-ryōri dinners when there's nothing important to celebrate, she thought to herself as she remembered the conversations she'd had with Yuriko earlier in the week.

—ɯ—

Haruka walked through her front door just after ten p.m. and found her mother waiting for her with a look of expectation on her face.

'Did he propose?' she asked with caution, noticing Haruka's glum expression. Haruka shook her head, upset that she may have disappointed her.

'Not to worry,' her mother said. 'I'm sure he'll propose when the time is right. When I was seeing your father, I had to wait a long time for him to propose. Life was different back then. I had to get to know his family a little bit and all sorts of arrangements had to be made. I'm sure there's nothing to worry about. He's probably going to wait until you move to Kyoto.'

'Thanks, I needed to hear that. I have to say goodnight. I'm exhausted and my feet are killing me in these heels – I'm going to bed,' said Haruka.'

'Goodnight, Haruka,' her mother replied.

—◊—

Yuriko texted Haruka twice the following day at work, asking her both times to visit her at home that night so as they could talk about the dinner date. Obviously, she hadn't talked to Jun when he'd arrived back at their house late the previous evening, thought Haruka. She knew for a fact that he'd planned to leave very early that morning to take the bullet train back to Kyoto.

It wasn't until about eight thirty that night that Haruka walked into Yuriko's room to find her exercising on her bike with the usual vigour. The excited look on her face showed Haruka that she expected her to announce that she was now engaged, but Haruka's tired and disappointed expression quickly told her otherwise.

'Did he ask you to marry him?' she asked as she peddled even faster.

'No, but I think he's just waiting for the right time,' Haruka replied reassuringly, as she took a seat in the pink-striped sofa chair. 'Well, he's returned to Kyoto now, so I'll have to wait and see what happens. I'd like to call and chat with him in Kyoto, but he never picks up his phone. It's strange – he hasn't even given me his home or work phone number, and so I usually have to wait until he comes to Ōfune to talk with him.'

'Oh don't worry about that,' replied Yuriko. 'He hardly ever picks up the phone when I call him, and he's rarely at home because he's busy all the time with work.'

'Hasn't he said anything to you about the engagement?' Haruka asked her.

'No, but I don't expect him to talk about it, Jun is really a very private person. He'd walk out of the room if I asked him about your relationship.'

Yuriko was now puffing quite a bit and slowed the bike down a little.

'Maybe he's going to wait until you move to Kyoto to propose,' said Yuriko.

'Yes, that's what my mother and I think,' Haruka replied.

'Your mother knows about this?' exclaimed Yuriko, looking at Haruka with a bewildered expression. 'I thought we made a promise that we weren't going to tell anyone else.'

Haruka couldn't tell her about how her mother had been depressed lately or about the money problems that her family wanted to keep a secret.

'I had to tell her, Yuriko, she really likes Jun and she's so happy for me.'

'I understand. It's difficult to keep this kind of news to yourself, especially when you're going to get such a beautiful ring. I would have told the whole world by now.'

'I want to change the subject – it's all getting a bit too much for me,' Haruka said to Yuriko. Haruka picked up one of her Hello Kitty toys and hugged it tight. 'Your room looks the same as it did when you were four years old.'

'Yes, but I like it like this. It's comforting.'

'Still, you could at least get rid of the children's books on the bookcase,' Haruka suggested.

'Yes, you're right,' said Yuriko. 'Maybe I should give all the toys and the books to the little girl from the family that lives on the other side of your house.'

'That's an excellent idea!' Haruka replied.

Haruka sat for a while in silence while Yuriko sped up again on her exercise bike and peddled like a mad woman. After ten minutes, she finally slowed down and jumped off the bike. She came over to kneel beside Haruka on the floor. The foundation that was pasted over her face was dripping with perspiration.

'Why don't I give you a makeover, Yuriko?' Haruka said to her. 'You have so many products in your bathroom that we could use. Come on – it will be fun.'

'Okay,' Yuriko replied hesitantly.

She sat on the bathroom stool and Haruka removed the thick spread of make-up with a Chanel cleanser. Most of her makeup and skincare products were bought from Chanel. Haruka wished she had such a selection to make up her face every morning.

Yuriko saw her reflection in the mirror and blushed. Now that Haruka had removed her foundation, you could see the pimples dotted all over her chin and forehead. Haruka smiled back at her with encouragement.

'I'm going to make you look even more beautiful. You know, your skin would clear up really quickly if you used less product and went for a more natural look,' Haruka said to her.

'You're probably right. But I use a lot of foundation as cover up. If I used less, my pimples would be more visible.'

'Not necessarily,' Haruka said to her. 'Have you been thinking about your two-timing ex-boyfriend much?' she asked Yuriko, changing the conversation hesitantly as she wiped a cotton ball soaked in clarifying lotion over her forehead.

'Not at all,' she replied.

'Really?' said Haruka, not truly convinced that she hadn't been thinking about him. Yuriko had always been a hopeless romantic and in the past, would often dwell on why a relationship worked for her or why it didn't go as she'd planned.

'I've moved on from thinking about Ryō,' she said. 'I'm completely over him.'

'Well, that's great,' Haruka replied, still not totally convinced she was over her feelings for him. Haruka remembered how Yuriko couldn't stop talking about him when they'd first met.

After applying the clarifying lotion, she chose to apply a light and gentle moisturiser from a choice of four different kinds of Chanel moisturisers that Yuriko had scattered on her bathroom counter. She followed this up with a dewy, luminous foundation, a mineral powder and a soft, peachy blusher. To finish the look, Haruka dabbed her eyelids with a creamy light brown eye shadow and lightly applied black mascara to her eyelashes before finally sweeping over a rose lip gloss onto her lips.

Haruka stood back to admire her work. The transformation was complete, and Yuriko looked much better, apart from her hair, which was looking a little lanky and in need of a good cut and blow dry.

'That looks fabulous. I actually look better without so much gunk on my face,' said Yuriko, looking at her face from one angle and then another in the mirror. 'Even my complexion looks clearer when I don't apply so much foundation and powder. I think I'm going to do my make up like this from now on.' Yuriko couldn't stop smiling at herself, very pleased with the end result.

'Yes, you look lovely,' Haruka said to her. 'I'm going to have to go home now because I'm starving.' Haruka picked up her bag and headed out of the bathroom towards Yuriko's bedroom door.

'Bye,' yelled out Yuriko, still sitting on the stool, not able to turn away from the mirror.

Haruka left Yuriko's house and walked home with thoughts of Jun and the engagement and the fact that he hadn't proposed. Her life was getting complicated waiting for Jun to pop the question. Later at home in her bedroom, she flicked through her bridal magazines again until she fell asleep. Haruka dreamt of a lavish wedding reception with lots of guests, a three-tiered wedding cake and classical music in the background, but it was not Jun holding her hand in the dream – it was Takashi.

CHAPTER 11

A good friend never offends

The weeks went by and Takashi spent his time trying to get through his studies. Although he studied until late, he would take a lot of breaks and it was sometimes two or three in the morning before he slept. He'd never been a morning person, and these late nights allowed him to get through his studies and then sleep in until noon.

He was wrapped up tightly in his futon one Monday morning in November when he was woken up by his mobile phone. It was vibrating against his chest. This sensation, as well as its ringing sound, penetrated his dreams and he pictured the bells of a temple clanging loudly over and over again. Takashi slowly drifted into reality and realised that there were no temples and it was the ring tone on his mobile phone that had woken him from his slumber. He exposed his face to the light of the morning and blinked at his mobile, trying to focus.

The time on the phone showed 10:19 a.m. Takashi picked it up and answered.

'Moshi moshi,' he said in a muffled voice as he sat up in order to wake himself up a little.

Masaya's shrill laughter came painfully through the phone, and Takashi held the handset an inch from his ear.

'You're studying too hard and putting too much emphasis on exams when you should be chasing girls,' he said. 'You're going to get ill looking at your textbooks all the time.'

Takashi rubbed his eyes and changed the conversation. 'Thanks for the sunglasses.'

'The sunglasses?' Masaya asked him innocently.

'From the Loft store.'

'No problem – just remember me when you're a top executive!' Masaya joked.

Takashi pulled himself up out of his bed and found himself laughing. Listening to Masaya, he really missed his high school friends.

They were talking for about fifteen minutes – well, actually Masaya was doing most of the talking, hardly breathing between sentences – when he paused for a second, seemingly lost in thought.

'I have a brilliant idea!' Masaya suddenly announced.

He'd decided, failing to wait for any agreement on Takashi's part, that they were going to head for Ginza that very afternoon to eat rice and noodle dishes at Kenji's restaurant. Takashi was half asleep and he couldn't get a word in. Before he knew it, he'd been informed that they were to meet in front of the Apple store in Ginza at one p.m., and that there would be no excuses.

The call ended and Takashi remained sitting in an upright stupor for a couple of minutes, looking at the textbooks scattered all over the floor beside his bed. He shook his head, knowing that he'd planned to spend the whole afternoon reading through next week's class notes, entitled "The Power of Semiotics and Branding Equity". However, it must have been his eagerness to see his friends or Masaya's voice beaming through the phone and his cheerful tone that changed Takashi's mind. He took a quick shower, but spent a little longer shaving to make sure he didn't nick himself and to get his sideburns just right. After that, he reorganised his study plan to leave a window of time open that would allow him to meet his mates in Ginza. For the first time in weeks, he felt a feeling of refreshment, even before he embarked on this afternoon adventure.

Before Takashi left his apartment, he checked his e-mails. His friend Akira, who was studying in America, had sent a group e-mail. It read:

Hi guys,

Sorry I haven't been in touch for a while. I've been travelling when I'm not studying. My girlfriend from Tokyo and I are going to New York next week. We're really looking forward to that. Please send me an e-mail when you have the time.

Akira

Takashi printed out a copy to show Masaya and hurried to the station to catch the train to Tokyo.

It was just after one p.m. when Takashi spotted Masaya leaning against the side of the Apple store, not far from Ginza train station. He followed his eye line and saw that he was checking out three girls, all wrapped up in cashmere coats and dripping with gold jewellery. Two of them were applying lipstick and the other was preening her hair. It was not unusual to see people posing in the middle of the street dressed as if they were about to go to a party or a wedding in this upmarket area of Tokyo.

Takashi was fully aware that Ginza was one of the busiest and most expensive shopping districts in the world. This was not a place he would normally frequent to go shopping; it was too pricey for his budget. He knew Haruka liked the area, though. In Ginza he could imagine her and Yuriko browsing through the luxurious Western brands they liked so much, like Gucci, Louis Vuitton, Dior and Chanel. The only shops that interested Takashi and his friends were Sony for the latest gadgets or the Apple store to check out the latest iPad and iPhone.

Even though the whole of the centre of Ginza breathed opulence and expense, affordable but very respectable eating holes could be found down the back streets, behind the department stores and designer boutiques. Kenji's eatery, Umi Gohan, could be defined as one of those establishments.

Takashi called out to Masaya whose face lit up when he saw him. Masaya ran over to catch up with him and they headed away from the main shopping avenue to the corner of Mihara and Azuma Street, where Umi Gohan was located. They found it quite easily, and Takashi and Masaya passed under the noren curtain and entered into a place full of young office ladies in suits and fashionable female sales assistants enjoying a meal.

The restaurant could easily seat twenty to thirty people at the tables that were lined up on the left hand side. On the right were nine stools where people could eat at the counter. This side bench was covered with several bottles of shochu rice wine, many bearing a tag labelled with the names of regular customers. Alongside the liquor were wooden stands filled with chopsticks and napkins. Next to those were condiments such as seven-spice shijimi and Kikkoman soy sauce. At the register was a Red Cross box for charity donations. The food was brought out from the back and into the middle of the restaurant from the kitchen.

There was only one businessman to be found inside sitting amongst a room full of young ladies: a nervous type eating at a furious pace, as if time was against him.

Masaya and Takashi watched Kenji come out from the back. He was dressed in black jeans and a steel grey polo neck top. Kenji turned to two of the young women, his arms laden with trays of steaming bowls of noodles, and gave each girl a short, cheeky smile as he passed them their lunch. It was then that he swung around and recognised them.

'What are you guys doing here?' Kenji asked, laughing. Just as quickly, he remembered where he was and offered them a table second from the front, next to the businessman. Takashi sat facing the window and Masaya sat opposite him.

'Good to see you here. Sit down, relax and take a look at our menu,' said Kenji.

They sat back to admire this small but neat and decidedly clean restaurant, of which Kenji was so proud. Once they were seated, Kenji went back to the kitchen.

'This place is nice. Look how clean it is. We should come here more often. How many times have you been here, Takashi?'

'Only once before,' he said.

'Just once?'

'Yes, just after it opened. And you, Masaya?'

'I brought Momo-chan here for lunch about a year ago. She raved about it afterwards. Every now and then she asks me if we can come back here.'

'Why didn't you bring her here today?' Takashi asked him.

'She's out shopping with a girlfriend trying to find things for the apartment.'

'Your apartment?'

'Yes. She says it looks too much like a bachelor pad.'

'She's right, you know.'

'Ha ha. I said to her that anything was fine as long as she didn't buy anything floral,' said Masaya.

'What did she say to that?' asked Takashi.

Masaya grinned and chuckled at Takashi. 'She didn't say anything. She threw a cushion at me!'

Takashi tried to imagine Masaya and Momo-chan having cushion fights. It would've been fun to watch.

They sat back and perused the restaurant for a couple of minutes.

'Have you heard from Akira?' Takashi suddenly asked Masaya.

'No, I haven't read my e-mails recently.'

Takashi took out the e-mail that he'd printed out from his pocket. 'Have a read of this,' he said, passing it over to Masaya.

Masaya read the e-mail. 'He doesn't say much. Who's the girlfriend?'

'I don't know. He doesn't say much about her at all. It must be serious.'

'I suppose so,' replied Masaya.

They each picked up a menu and eagerly studied it. There was a terrific choice of dishes. They both opted for the lunch sets, but couldn't decide which one. Masaya was looking at the lunchtime options and had the choice of a tuna mince dish, baked spicy tuna, a shellfish set, Chinese style noodles or a tuna sashimi. He finally decided on the baked spicy tuna noodle set. Takashi was looking at the Maguro Tuna board and chose a raw tuna rice dish called Teka Donburi.

The meal arrived, and they thanked Kenji. He turned and went back into the kitchen again and Masaya lowered his voice and indicated to Takashi to tilt his head closer.

'Have a look – in the last fifteen minutes, four tables have turned over customers and eight girls have been replaced by another eight young girls and a lot of them are very pretty!'

Takashi turned and looked around the room. Masaya was right. This place was full of gorgeous girls in suits and designer clothes. Masaya and Takashi looked at each other with a knowing smile. Kenji had been one of the most popular boys in high school, and he'd often helped them find dates. Kenji had obviously been placed as the front man for the restaurant and the combination of his rugged good looks and his charming personality was drawing in the female workers from the surrounding area.

'No wonder Kenji is always saying how much he loves his job!' Masaya said to Takashi.

'Maybe I should get a job here!' Takashi joked.

Kenji's father was American and his mother was Japanese. He'd taken after his father, in that he was very tall and towered over most other Japanese men. His shoulders were broad and he was as tough as beef jerky, thanks to long hours working out in the gym when he was younger. Kenji had the physical attributes of a male model. He had an olive complexion, as he often spent weekends in the surf. His hair was as black as charcoal and he had a curl that licked his forehead and swept over a roguishly handsome face. However, it was his angelic smile that all the girls commented on.

Takashi was still thinking about his friend Kenji and his good fortune when Masaya suddenly turned to attract the attention of the businessman who'd been eating alone. He was just about to leave, and he was startled by Masaya's call.

'Hey, wait up,' Masaya cried out to him. Masaya pointed in the direction of the businessman's forehead. The man turned and almost looked afraid of Masaya. He'd obviously sweated over his hot meal and he had a piece of paper napkin left stuck to his forehead. He'd probably wiped his brow after his meal, and his oily skin had caused it to stick. He removed the napkin and the fear on his face quickly turned to gratitude after his embarrassment had passed. Having checked his forehead again, he hurried out, his head down and his shoulders hunched over.

Masaya turned to Takashi and said in a hushed voice. 'So tell me, what happened to you and Haruka? I thought everything was going well with you two until I saw Jun getting friendly with her at the café in Daikanyama.'

'I thought everything was going well, too. I was sure we were starting to get closer, but now I'm not so sure,' Takashi replied. He picked up the seven-spice shijimi and started stamping it on the table in short bursts.

'What happened?' Masaya asked.

'Oh, come on Masaya – you've seen it for yourself. She's obviously more interested in Jun and I'm beginning to understand why. For starters, he's rich, tall, better looking than me, and obviously a lot more charming. We used to talk on the phone every second day. I don't know what to do. From the very first day I saw her at the lecture, I thought that she was the one – and I thought I was getting closer to her, but….'

Masaya interrupted. 'I know you really like her, Takashi. Every time I tried to call your mobile a few months ago you were on the phone talking with her.'

'Exactly, and now I'm lucky if I get to speak to her once a week,' said Takashi. He put the seven-spice shijimi back next to the soy sauce.

'I don't understand it, either. When I saw her with Jun, it seemed to me that she was just being polite to him. The problem is that she's female and there's no way to figure out what a woman is thinking,' said Masaya.

'Well, I have to take it the way I see it – and I don't think she's interested in me anymore.'

'That's rubbish, Takashi. Jun might be able to fool the girls, but it didn't take long for me to see through his pretentious exterior and it won't be long before Haruka sees this, too. If you want me to be honest, I still think she really likes you and Jun is just clouding her judgement.'

'Well, time will tell.'

'Where's he from? I've never seen him before and I've never heard Haruka mention him.'

'Jun's from Kyoto – he's Yuriko's cousin.'

'I think the stress of your exams and this business with Haruka is getting to you – you even have a couple of pimples on your forehead. I know you must be really stressed if your skin's bad,' said Masaya.

Takashi nodded. He hadn't wanted this conversation to crop up. He cut it short by taking out his packet of Mild Seven cigarettes and offering Masaya one. They smoked in silence for about five minutes before beckoning Kenji to come over and join them.

'Thanks Kenji, that was delicious,' Masaya and Takashi said in unison.

Kenji sat down at the table with them. All of the customers had now finished their meals and had left to return to their workplaces, except for one stylish lady at the back of the restaurant. She was wearing a sexy Junko Shimada navy peplum jacket and matching skirt.

'You certainly get to meet a lot of beautiful girls working here, don't you, Kenji?' said Masaya.

'Yes I certainly do,' replied Kenji. 'But I tell you what, boys – they wear me out, and not in a good way. I've dated eight customers in the past month.'

'Eight girls!'Takashi exclaimed.

'Yes, eight girls, Takashi, but they're mostly shallow and insincere. I've yet to meet a girl that doesn't expect everything done for her and who doesn't gets irritable and frustrated if I ask her to do something for me. I'd like to meet a kind and sincere girl, but I don't think Ginza is the right area if you want to meet someone like that.'

'I feel so sorry for you,' Takashi said, mocking his misfortune. His sarcasm earned him a playful punch in the arm from Kenji.

'Tell me, Kenji, what's the recipe for that noodle dish?' Masaya asked, changing the subject. 'I could use that on my menu at the tavern.'

Kenji winked at Masaya. 'Family secret – can't tell you that Masaya – but you're welcome to eat here anytime.' Kenji smiled to himself and left them to wander over and charm the attractive woman sitting by herself at the back of the restaurant.

'He's a cheeky fellow, isn't he?' Masaya said to Takashi, not one bit bothered about the recipe.

Before they left, Masaya paid Kenji's mother ¥5,000 to reserve his own bottle of Miyazaki shochu rice wine and promised to revisit one evening over the next few months with a group of people to drink it and enjoy the food again. In return, Kenji wouldn't let them pay for their lunches at the register, even though they tried to insist on paying several times over. They gratefully left the restaurant, both of them having fully enjoyed a great afternoon.

Umi Gohan was conveniently situated near the corner of Mihara and Azuma Street, behind Mitsukoshi department store, so they decided to do a little window shopping before they went on their separate ways to head home.

'Let's go and have a look at the Apple store,' suggested Masaya.

'You don't need a computer, do you?' asked Takashi.

'No,' he answered. 'But I'd like to take a look at the new models.'

'Okay, but then I'd like to go home. It's freezing outside,' Takashi said through chattering teeth.

CHAPTER 12

A true friend is a great treasure

It was nine p.m. when Takashi returned to his apartment. The room was cold, and he changed into an old grey sweater and turned on the kotatsu under the coffee table. He placed his hands under the thick cover that spread over the table and held his hands close to the warmth of the kotatsu's heater to heat up his fingers and toes that were a little bit numb from his brisk walk home. Takashi decided to watch TV, as he was too tired to study and he kept telling himself that it was too late anyway to start any serious work.

He started watching the repeat of a soccer game, but he knew what the result was, and it wasn't long before his mind began to wander. He lay back and now that his hands had lost their frosty tingle, he stretched out. His legs were crossed and the lower part of his body was covered under the table. His upper body rested on the floor against his pillow. His hands were under his head as he looked up at the ceiling.

Against the bleating tone of the umpire's voice coming from the television, his thoughts drifted. He smiled as he remembered Kenji's face when he first saw them at the restaurant and Masaya's friendly conversation throughout the meal. Takashi really enjoyed Masaya's company and he thought of him as a great friend. It wasn't long before his thoughts turned back to the conversation that he'd shared with him about Haruka. He would have given anything to tell Masaya that his relationship with Haruka was going well and he was really happy – but he'd been honest and ended up looking to him for support instead – and now his good friend was left feeling sorry for him.

Over the last couple of weeks, he'd found himself thinking about Haruka more often than usual, and he couldn't put her out of his mind. The day before, Takashi had even thrown his textbook at the wall in frustration after thinking about her for a full half hour. He often had to force himself to think about something else, because daydreaming about Haruka left him feeling like there was a big gap in his life that couldn't be filled unless she was part of it. Takashi deliberately forced his thoughts back to his friend Masaya.

Masaya and Takashi had been through a lot together, and Takashi had always respected him for being himself. He'd never been really good looking or even average-looking. Masaya was a bit dumpy in the face and he had scars left over from early acne problems, so he always maintained a five o'clock shadow to hide this. He wore his hair quite long at the neck and coloured it brown. His hair suited him a lot better when it was really short, but Masaya always wore it just how he liked it. He liked to be trendy, never listening to how other people would prefer him to appear.

Takashi thought that Masaya's most admirable and most redeeming quality was his personality. His big face framed a wide grin that made him look like a loveable cartoon character. He had a twinkle in his eyes and a robust voice that would sometimes turn into a wheezy chuckle from too many cigarettes. He always made everyone smile. It was for these reasons that people were instantly drawn to him. He convulsed with glee over the simplest things and he often dramatised the most mundane situations so that you were captivated by his stories. As well as this, Masaya had a keen sense of style, and Kenji and Takashi always liked having him around when they went shopping.

Masaya had met his girlfriend Momo-chan in high school. They'd been dating for about two years and Momo-chan was also a character in her own right. You instantly recognised her when she was in the room, because her voice had a high-pitched nasal twang. Momo-chan was eighteen years old and reminded Takashi of the type of girl you saw hosting music programmes on TV. Her original sense of style was kind of Lolita-cum-rock-cum-punk-cum kewpie doll. The last time he saw her, she had her hair in braids that were wound around the side of her head in the style of Princess Leia from *Star Wars*. Her make-up had consisted of blue glitter around the eyes and bright red lipstick just covering the middle of her lips, like a geisha.

That day, now long gone by, she'd been wearing a denim jacket covered in studs, a T-shirt that had an image of Led Zeppelin printed on the back, a very short denim skirt edged in black lace, pink stockings that stretched up just over her knees and ridiculously high platform shoes. Takashi's mouth had fallen open when he saw her, but that happened every time he saw her in a different outfit and Momo-chan obviously adored everyone's reactions to what she wore.

Masaya and Momo-chan were very close, but since he'd bought the bar, he'd been extremely busy and hadn't wanted her to distract him at work. However, he often encouraged Kenji and Takashi to drop in for a drink and something to eat. Momo-chan respected his wishes and they mostly just met during the day or on Sunday and Monday night when the tavern was closed. Now that they were living together, Takashi thought he'd probably see her most days but when he wasn't working.

Just before he fell asleep, Takashi decided that he would get in touch with Kenji and arrange to return the favour and visit Masaya at his tavern in Shimokitazawa. He dialled his number. The phone rang several times before he picked it up.

'Kenji, it's me, Takashi.'

Kenji yawned. 'Oh hi, good to see you today,' he drawled in a sleepy voice.

'Sorry did I wake you?' Takashi asked.

'Yes, but that's cool.'

'Masaya and I had such a good time today. What do you think of us all going to drink at his tavern in Shimokitazawa next weekend?'

'Let's surprise him,' said Kenji.

'Yes, that would be fun.'

'Okay, let's make it next Saturday,' Kenji said.

'Great, I'll ring around and get a few people to come.'

'Nice one, I'll meet you outside Shimokitazawa station at six.'

'Sounds good. Are you going back to sleep?' Takashi asked.

'Of course,' Kenji replied.

CHAPTER 13

He that can have patience can have what he will

On the first Saturday in December, the whole gang, except for Momo-chan, who had declined the invitation, decided to meet and surprise Masaya at his tavern, named Enya.

Haruka, Yuriko and Takashi were waiting outside the south exit at Shimokitazawa station for Kenji. It was six p.m. and they were all wearing gloves, hats and scarves. They knew that Masaya's tavern was pretty laid back; so all three of them were in jeans and casual sweaters underneath warm coats. It was less than 5° Celsius outside and the frosty air made their eyes glossy and their cheeks rosy. They rubbed their hands together to try and keep warm, blowing into their cupped palms every couple of minutes and stamping their feet to keep the circulation going.

'Is Kenji coming by train?' asked Yuriko. She was dressed in a suede jacket and tight blue jeans that evening. Takashi was surprised to see that she didn't have one label showing that night, and her makeup looked much nicer and more natural than usual. He thought to himself that she looked quite pretty for a change.

'No, he's driving his car here,' Takashi replied. 'He said he'd park near the station and meet us at the south exit. He's probably looking for somewhere to park.'

Yuriko turned to face Haruka. 'Have you met him, Haruka? Do you know what he looks like?' she asked her.

'Yes, I met him a few years ago,' said Haruka. 'He's very nice. He looks like a model. Has he done any modelling, Takashi?'

'No, he doesn't have the patience or the vanity for that,' Takashi replied.

'Will he bring someone? He has a lot of girlfriends, doesn't he?' asked Haruka.

'I think so,' Takashi said.

'So he's a bit of a player?' Yuriko asked, seemingly annoyed.

'No, I wouldn't say that … there's Kenji,' said Takashi, pointing in the direction of the train station. The others turned around and saw him coming quickly towards them. He was easy to recognise because of his height: he towered above all the other commuters and shoppers bursting from the various platforms and heading out of the station.

It was immediately obvious that Kenji was not alone, and their eyes bulged. Kenji, dressed in a brown leather jacket and black jeans, had his arm casually slung around a woman. The closer they got, the more obvious it became that this woman was quite a lot older and very sophisticated. Kenji reached the three of them and introduced the woman as Akiko. He gave Takashi a friendly punch, because his eyes were travelling slowly up from her stilettos to her face.

'Have you been waiting long?' Kenji asked them.

'Only about ten minutes,' said Takashi. 'Kenji, you know Haruka, and this is her friend Yuriko.'

'Nice to meet you, Yuriko,' said Kenji.

Akiko lifted her leg like a deer and removed a pebble from her stiletto. Takashi marvelled at the way that she could balance on one foot with so much ease.

'Is Masaya's tavern far from here?' Haruka asked him.

'No. Follow me, everyone. We'll be there in five minutes,' Takashi said.

'Good – I'm freezing,' said Yuriko.

'Yes, it is cold isn't it?' Takashi said, 'but I'd stand for hours in this weather to wait to eat at Masaya's tavern. The food and the atmosphere are fantastic there.'

They headed down the street. Takashi walked slightly ahead, like a tour guide, and the other four followed. They had to wind their way past the shops that were still open. There was a buzz of people everywhere.

Haruka, Yuriko and Takashi couldn't help stealing glances at Akiko on the way to the bar. She was obviously expensively dressed and extremely stylish, but she looked a little out of place for Shimokitazawa. This town was full of students and jeans were without doubt the uniform of choice around here. Akiko was wearing a tight, fitted navy leather jacket and matching micro mini skirt with bare legs that managed her high heels with unbelievable ease. Takashi thought that she could easily have been mistaken for a high-class hostess from Roppongi who entertained in bars.

They walked past a McDonald's and a Las Vegas Pachinko parlour before they reached Masaya's tavern. His izakaya was situated in a side street off the main strip. A huge neon light announced the tavern's name – 'Enya'. This was easy to see from the main road. A glowing lantern with the same name hung proudly by the entrance.

A waitress greeted them at the counter, which was decorated with artificial flames and a fish tank bursting with bright silver fish. The tavern had a very relaxed feel about it, and that was perfect for an izakaya. They knew that it would be a fun evening, and they would soon be enjoying tasty appetisers and plenty to drink. They were led to one of the booths lined with leather lounges and a solid wooden table, just right for five people at a squeeze. Above them, a huge round paper lantern glowed, a buzzer was conveniently fixed to the wall for them to call the waitress at any time and the menus were laid out waiting for them to order throughout the evening.

Haruka removed her heavy wool coat. Underneath, she was wearing a black cardigan and a silky, white blouse over faded bootleg jeans. She looked relaxed and happy.

They ordered beer, shochu rice wine and soft drinks between them. Kenji and Akiko had the honours of ordering the food for all of them and soon they were sinking their teeth into appetisers such as spinach, tomato and bacon salad, sashimi, a variety of grilled yakitori chicken pieces on skewers, pan-fried pepper steak, and shrimps with mayonnaise as well as fried squid.

Not knowing that they were there, Masaya walked past the table and did a double take. He was so surprised to see them that he fell back a few steps and tripped on the partition between the booths. He swiftly jumped back up again and everyone applauded him for his quick recovery. Masaya had obviously never expected his Ginza surprise to be reciprocated.

'I can't believe it. You nearly didn't recognise us,' Takashi teased him.

Masaya nodded towards Akiko. 'I saw her first,' he said, 'But then I heard Kenji's laugh, and it made me stop when I recognised his voice. Good to see you all.'

Masaya surveyed the group and then rested his eyes on Akiko. 'Isn't anyone going to introduce me?' he asked.

'This is Akiko, Kenji's friend,' said Takashi.

Akiko looked directly at Masaya. Her long stare made him blush. 'How is the food?' Masaya stammered, pointing at their table.

'Delicious,' Takashi replied.

'Great. Please enjoy. I'll come back later. I have to see what's happening in the kitchen.' Masaya said. He turned and scurried out towards the back of the tavern.

—ɱ—

Halfway through the meal, Takashi pulled Kenji aside. 'Who is this woman?' he asked him. 'Is it your new girlfriend and by the way, how old is she?'

'She comes into my restaurant every week by herself and so I asked her out a couple of weeks ago, and we've been dating ever since,' replied Kenji. 'She works as a personal assistant for a fashion company in Ginza.'

'She's almost old enough to be your mum,' Takashi teased Kenji.

He laughed. 'Don't be silly, she's only thirty-three,' he said.

'Only thirty-three,' Takashi exclaimed as his mouth fell open.

'I like her maturity,' Kenji replied, looking a bit awkward. They stood for a couple of minutes in silence.

'I have some exciting news to tell you, Takashi,' said Kenji, taking a picture of a motorbike out of his pocket and handing it to him to inspect. 'I'm buying a high-performance Ducati bike in the morning – take a look at this,' he said.

Takashi looked at the speed machine on the page in awe. 'That's a very cool bike, Kenji,' he said, wishing he could own this beautiful red piece of machinery.

'I should be able to get to work and back home quicker on that, don't you think?' said Kenji, taking the picture back and sliding it into his back pocket.

'You mean you'll be able to see more girlfriends in one day, speeding through Tokyo!' Takashi replied.

'Talking of girls, what's happening with Haruka? Something has to happen soon. I'm tired of hearing you say, 'we're just friends',' Kenji said to Takashi.

'I can never find the right time to be alone with her and give her a kiss,' he replied with a long face.

'You don't wait for the right time – you decide that you're going to kiss her and you kiss her. It's that easy. Now I want you to make it your number one mission to kiss her before the night ends. You could even make her jealous by flirting with my date. I don't mind a bit,' Kenji said with a broad smile.

'What seems so easy to you is a lot more difficult for me, Kenji,' Takashi replied.

Whether Kenji was half-joking or half-serious was difficult to tell, but Takashi realised he had to take action and soon, or he was going to miss out on the golden opportunity. Kenji gave him a big grin and a wink and they returned to the table.

Akiko was sitting on one side waiting for Kenji and Haruka and Yuriko were asking her all kinds of make-up and fashion questions. By the way they were speaking to her and taking mental notes, they both obviously thought that she was stunning and wanted to know all her secrets. Takashi looked at Akiko and he thought her make-up was really overdone, as well as her clothes, and he was not happy that she was taking up so much of Haruka's attention. They'd all had a few drinks and Takashi kept waiting for the right moment to move in and intercept their conversation as he sat beside Haruka.

Suddenly, they all turned around and looked at the booth beside them. Loud laughs and a commotion were coming from that direction. Three foreigners, talking loudly in English and obviously quite inebriated and in high spirits, were sitting themselves down at the adjacent table. Takashi had learnt English at school, but he couldn't understand very much of their conversation at all. He turned his head again and saw three young foreign men in rugby shirts and ripped jeans laughing and shoving each other's shoulders. One of the boys had golden-coloured hair and freckles. He'd never seen hair so light, except on television.

'Look at the guy with the golden hair,' Takashi said to Kenji, nodding at the young man. 'I've seen a lot of blonde foreigners at the Yokosuka Naval Base near my parents' house, but I've never seen anyone as fair as him.'

'I wish my hair was blonde like that,' Kenji replied with eyes wide open.

The golden-haired foreign boy made his way over to their table. Takashi looked at Kenji. He thought that maybe the boy understood Japanese and had heard what they'd said.

'*Does anyone speak English?*' the golden-haired boy asked them in English, carefully enunciating each word for their benefit.

Yuriko pulled at Haruka's shirt. 'You work for an English conversation school. You speak to him,' she said to Haruka.

'*Yes,*' Haruka said in English to the foreign boy.

'*We ... do ... not ... understand ... Japanese,*' the golden haired boy said carefully to Haruka.

'*Ye ... s,*' said Haruka.

'*We … don't understand… the … menu. It's … in Japanese … what should … we eat*?' he said in English that even Takashi could comprehend.

'*I … understand*,' said Haruka to the foreign boy. She pressed the buzzer for the waitress, who appeared immediately.

'Do you have an English menu?' Haruka asked her.

'No,' the waitress replied, looking at the golden-haired boy with a worried expression.

The foreign boy pointed at the food on their table, circling the top of each plate with his forefinger. '*We will eat this*,' he announced.

Haruka nodded.

'They'll eat the same food as us,' Haruka said to the waitress.

'*The same food – yes?*' Haruka asked the foreign boy in English.

'*Yes… yes*,' he replied. The golden-haired boy looked very pleased with himself. He returned to his table, and his friends clapped and patted him on the back.

'Well done!' the whole group said to Haruka in unison, and she blushed from all the compliments.

It was then that Takashi hoped to have a word with Akiko in his attempt to make Haruka jealous, at the same time hoping that it would not backfire.

'Hey, Akiko – everyone has been commenting on your hair. May I say it really is very beautiful. Maybe you should try modelling,' he said trying not to cringe, thinking his comments may have come across a little bit too heavy.

However, Akiko seemed very pleased and offered Takashi a beaming smile as she placed her hand on his knee and said, 'Oh Kenji, your friend is *sooo* cute.'

With her hand on his knee, Takashi's whole body tensed up, and he couldn't utter a word. Looking at Haruka, he noticed her eyes travel back and forth from Akiko's face to her hand on his knee and then back to her face.

Did I notice a slight glimmer of jealousy in her eyes? Takashi thought to himself. He still couldn't talk or move a muscle, but he spotted Kenji in the corner having a marvellous time watching the whole scenario. Akiko removed her hand from Takashi's knee and he blew a sigh of relief.

Yuriko jumped up and tried to squeeze in beside Takashi and Kenji. 'How long have you two known each other?' Yuriko asked them.

'About five or six years,' replied Kenji. 'We went to school together.'

Takashi wasn't in the mood to make small talk with Yuriko, so he excused himself and went to the bathroom, leaving Yuriko to chat with Kenji. A few minutes later, when he returned to the table, he sat down again next to Haruka. Everyone was talking about what they should do for New Year's Eve. Masaya had come over to take a break. It was not so busy at that time and many of his customers had left.

'Let's drive to the Izu Peninsula for New Year's Eve to watch the sunrise,' Masaya said, topping up their drinks.

Masaya had recently been given a brand new Honda Prelude, and Kenji and Takashi had both been eager to take a ride in it.

'Sounds like a terrific idea,' everybody agreed.

'My older brother Taroo has a BMW, and he'd be happy to take some of us up there,' Yuriko said.

Takashi's eyes lit up. BMW was his favourite car. *That's the smartest thing that's come out of her mouth since I met her*, Takashi thought. If only he owned an amazing car like a BMW or a Porsche, maybe then he would have more opportunities to be with Haruka.

'How about my brother and I take Haruka and Takashi?' Yuriko said.

'And I'll take Momo-chan, Kenji and Akiko,' Masaya added.

Everyone ordered another drink and they toasted this idea.

It was getting late and Kenji offered to take Yuriko and Akiko home. He was clever enough to suggest that Takashi look after Haruka.

Takashi turned to her. 'It's really late, Haruka ... it'll be light in a few hours. Would you like to wait at my place until the morning?'

'Okay,' she replied sheepishly.

Takashi couldn't tell whether she blushed deeply because she was flattered when she said this one simple word – which made his heart beat faster – or whether the colour of her cheeks was the effect of the alcohol.

The two of them called a taxi and shared a breezy cab ride back to Takashi's apartment in Kawasaki. Haruka was cold and curled up close to him in the back of the taxi as they drove through the streets. He put his arm around her and, unaware of the driver, they stared out at the lights against the dark night. He felt like he could've held her like this until the morning.

But back at the apartment it was Takashi's turn to blush. He opened the door and the smell of cigarettes filled the small room. He'd forgotten to tidy up before he'd left to go to Shimokitazawa.

Haruka untied her shoes and Takashi grabbed clothes and underwear and shoved them under the bed. They took off their coats and Haruka offered to make them green tea. Sitting down at the table, Takashi noticed that the cigarette stench was coming from the ashtray he'd left full of butt ends. He quickly emptied it outside.

Back inside, he slipped a Ryuichi Sakamoto CD into the stereo. The gentle, instrumental backdrop created a dreamlike mood.

'The food was delicious tonight, didn't you think so?' said Haruka.

'Yes, it was,' Takashi replied. The scent of her familiar jasmine perfume filled him with desire.

She poured water into the kettle. 'Do you have any biscuits or crackers?' she asked.

'Yes, I have some rice crackers,' he said. He took some rice crackers from an open packet and put them on a plate on the coffee table.

'Did you notice Yuriko had only one yakitori stick throughout the whole meal tonight?' said Haruka.

'I saw her pretending to eat. She kept playing with her food,' Takashi replied. 'What's wrong with her?'

'She has a serious problem. There's lots of reasons she won't eat,' said Haruka.

'Would you like to watch television?' Takashi asked her. He wanted to change the subject. He knew that talking about Yuriko would only depress Haruka.

'No, the music's fine,' Haruka replied softly. She'd finished making the tea and she handed him his cup.

'Are you cold?' asked Takashi. 'I'll turn on the kotatsu.'

Takashi flicked the switch on to heat up their feet. His toes were still numb from the taxi ride. The driver had kept the front passenger window slightly open in the car, and it hadn't occurred to him to ask him to close it. Haruka nibbled on a rice cracker.

'I was really impressed by the way you spoke English tonight,' Takashi said to her.

'You're too kind. I don't think my English is very good.'

Haruka finished her cracker and moved closer to him. She'd taken off her cardigan and the silk on her sleeve brushed against his right arm. Her signature scent of jasmine was more intoxicating than anything that he'd sipped earlier. He reached over to get her a cushion, but when he turned back to her, she was lying down, and she'd curled into a ball obviously falling asleep. Takashi gently placed the cushion under her head. Putting his arm around her shoulders, he pulled her towards him and kissed her cheek. She took his hand and squeezed it gently. He waited, hoping she would return his kiss, but she didn't stir. They went to sleep. Takashi would have liked to take it further, but he was content just to hold her while she slept until the morning.

Takashi woke up at about ten a.m. and saw that he was alone. He looked at the nicotine-stained walls. Just a few hours earlier, they had been the only witness to his affections. Memories of the night before were so hazy. Being there with Haruka was like a dream. A note on the table read:

"Thank you – I had a great time – love Haruka."

He smiled, remembering how lovely it was to hold her all night.

An hour or two passed, and he decided to call Kenji to tell him the news about the previous night with Haruka. He was hoping he could share with him his ever-growing feeling towards her, but Kenji didn't pick up his phone when he called. *Of course*, Takashi thought to himself, *he was probably having lunch with his family.* For a moment, he'd forgotten it was Sunday.

Takashi sent him a text message: "Everything went well with Haruka – did you stay at Akiko's?"

Before long, Kenji sent a message back: "I'm happy it's working out with Haruka. I was a bit tired of Akiko, so I took her straight home. I made sure Yuriko got home safely as well. I'm having lunch with the family now. Let's speak soon."

Takashi thought of his family enjoying their Sunday in Yokosuka. He'd been meaning to go and see them again for a while now. He decided that it would be best if he left it for a while. His father liked spending his Sundays sleeping off a busy week, and his mother would have felt obliged to cook for him if he'd shown up.

CHAPTER 14

A precipice in front, a wolf behind

It was just before nine p.m. on the thirty-first of December, the last night of the year. Takashi was sitting on the bottom step that led up to his apartment. He was waiting for Yuriko's older brother to pick him up to take them all to Izu for their New Year's celebration. The cold was brushing against his cheeks, but it felt good. He thought that he must have looked a bit silly sitting by himself all wrapped up in layers of clothing with a wide grin on his face. He was looking forward to spending several hours in the back of a BMW with Haruka next to him, as they were chauffeur-driven by Yuriko's brother Taroo to the peninsula to watch the sunrise.

Soon a pair of bright headlights came towards him. Takashi jumped up and watched the white BMW approaching approvingly. Yuriko and her brother smiled at him from the front seats. He craned his neck to look for Haruka in the back. He was happy to see her sitting in the middle back seat. He'd been half afraid that she wouldn't have been able to make it.

Takashi took off his North Face puffer jacket and climbed into the car. Moving Haruka's bag to sit down, he saw *him*. The colour drained from his face. White as a ghost and with a huge lump forming in his throat, he croaked a 'Happy New Year.'

'Jun is staying with my family again for the New Year and so we invited him along,' Yuriko said hesitantly.

'Oh,' said Takashi, almost choking on this one monosyllable.

'Hi,' said Haruka, before turning away from Takashi to face Jun. Haruka started describing the Izu Peninsula to him.

For some reason, Takashi wasn't angry at that point; he was just confused. *Why didn't anyone told me that Jun was coming along?* he thought to himself, wondering if Haruka really did care about him and if the evening they'd spent together had meant nothing to her. *Is that why she'd left in the morning without a word? Did her note mean that she cared about me but she really wanted to be with Jun*? The vein in his head was thumping, and he opened the window a little to get some air. He really wanted a cigarette.

'Good to see you again,' said Jun in a hollow voice.

'Likewise,' Takashi mumbled back. He thought Haruka might reach over and take his hand. He kept hoping for a while that she would. This would prove to Takashi that Jun was not her boyfriend. But Haruka's hands remained tightly clasped on her lap. To Takashi's disappointment, several times throughout the journey he saw her hand brush against Jun's knee, too many times for it to be natural. This trip was not working in his favour at all.

Everyone remained silent for the most part of the journey. They drove like this for hours towards Izu, listening to an Ayumi Hamasaki CD.

What was supposed to be the highlight of the year for Takashi was slowly becoming his worst night of the year, and the feeling he'd experienced as he'd waited on the steps of his apartment had now been turned inside out, along with his stomach.

They reached the peninsula at about four a.m. and met up with Kenji, Masaya, Momo-chan and Akiko.

Takashi walked away from the group, not in a good mood. He watched Masaya and Momo-chan, who looked so happy together with their arms around each other, leaning against Masaya's car. Taroo was brushing leaves off his BMW and a couple of feet away from him, Haruka was talking to Akiko and also Jun, who looked very pleased with himself for having the full attention of both girls. Yuriko was deep in conversation with Kenji, who was facing Takashi about five feet away.

After a few minutes of feeling sorry for himself, Takashi felt uncomfortable just standing alone away from the group, and he beckoned to Kenji to come over. He saw him wave and nodded. Kenji knew by the look on Takashi's face, even in the dark, that he was unhappy and he was good enough to leave Yuriko near the car to come and sit with him on a huge rock on the side of the mountain. Takashi looked straight ahead. He could hear the bubbling waves crashing against the rocks below. The smell of sea salt and damp leaves filled his nostrils.

Takashi and Kenji sat together on the rock in silence for a few minutes watching Momo-chan bring back a box of chocolate Pocky sticks from the car. They looked on as she passed them around the group.

'How can I compete with someone like him?' Takashi suddenly protested, nodding towards Jun.

'What are you talking about, Takashi? He's a smug snob with no personality.'

Takashi peeled off his right glove, pulled out a packet of Mild Sevens from the front right pocket of his jeans and lit a cigarette. 'He might be a snob, but Haruka's parents think he's great. I haven't got a chance in the world.'

'You're too hard on yourself,' Kenji said.

Takashi flicked his ash with force. 'Why does this have to be so difficult?' he asked as he scratched his left ear nervously. Takashi flicked his ash again, so hard this time that he scratched off half the stub.

'I suppose that sometimes you have to go to hell to appreciate heaven,' Kenji replied.

This made Takashi smile. Every now and then, Kenji came out with the wisest comments. *No wonder the girls find him so charming*, Takashi thought to himself. If anyone was going to be there for him, he was glad it was

Kenji. They sat together silently for a while. Takashi was using Kenji as an emotional crutch. He hated himself for needing any sort of support.

'Did you get that Ducati motorbike we were talking about at Masaya's tavern, Kenji?' Takashi asked Kenji, secretly hoping he might be able to take it for a spin.

'I certainly did.'

'How is it?' Takashi asked.

'It rides like a dream.'

There were about twenty-five people waiting for the sunrise at that point on the mountain. A few metres away, the rest of the group were standing together, looking uncomfortable. Only Momo-chan, who was too young to notice or to understand the situation, was trying to persuade Masaya to play a game of rock-paper-scissors. There was only one chocolate Pocky stick left and they used the game to decide who should have it. Momo-chan beat Masaya with a rock over scissors, but they shared the last stick together.

Akiko, dressed in liquid leather again, was talking to Jun. Even Kenji and Takashi could hear them talking. Haruka and Yuriko also stopped to listen to their conversation.

'You're from Kyoto?' Akiko asked Jun.

'Yes,' he replied. 'I was invited to a couple of parties in Kyoto, but I decided to come to Tokyo instead. Excuse me, but if you don't mind me asking, Akiko, how old are you?' Jun said, flicking his hair casually.

'A little bit older than Kenji.'

'Really? I thought you were a lot older,' he said, but Akiko ignored his rudeness. 'Aren't you cold in that short skirt?' Jun continued.

'Akiko might not be very warm, but she looks really trendy in that skirt,' said Yuriko, smiling at Akiko.

'Leather skirts are fashionable?' asked Jun sarcastically.

Akiko scowled at Jun. This time, she really didn't appreciate his sarcasm.

Jun saw that he'd upset her and he tried to turn it around. 'I'm sorry – I didn't mean to be rude,' he said to Akiko sincerely.

Everyone listening looked at Jun with disbelief. It was unbelievable that Jun was actually showing concern for someone. Akiko returned his apology with a warm and sympathetic smile.

Kenji and Takashi went to rejoin the group. Takashi wanted to pull Haruka to one side and talk with her, but it didn't seem like the right time or place. They stood there for about two hours waiting for the sunrise. Just before light, Momo-chan and Yuriko began talking about the singer that they'd been listening to in the car on the way up to Izu.

'I just love Ayumi Hamasaki,' said Momo-chan. 'Do you like her music?'

'Oh yes,' replied Yuriko. 'I have every one of her albums. She's my favourite pop star.'

Jun rolled his eyes. He was obviously not a fan of Ayumi Hamasaki, but Momo-chan and Yuriko ignored him.

'Yuriko, don't you think she's the most sincere famous person you've ever listened to?'

'Oh yes,' replied Yuriko. 'She's so honest, Momo-chan. Everything she says comes straight from the heart, doesn't it? And don't you think she sets so many fashion trends? She's constantly reinventing herself. I'm always looking to see what she's going to wear next.'

Suddenly Masaya interjected and said, 'Gosh, I wish there was a MOS Burger right up here on the peninsula – I'm starving.'

'You're so right, Masaya,' said Momo-chan, reaching over and giving her boyfriend a hug. 'I think I could eat a teriyaki chicken burger, a MOS rice burger and a spicy chilli dog all at once, and I'd still have room for a hot cocoa!'

'Well, I bet I could wolf down a spicy cheese burger, a fish burger, a straight chilli dog, and onion rings and let me see – corn soup!' Masaya retorted with a chuckle as he wrapped his arms tightly around Momo-chan.

'That's disgusting,' said Jun. 'Fast food is so greasy and bad for you and it gives you pimples.'

'Oh shut up, Jun, everyone loves MOS Burger. You're no fun at all,' barked Kenji as he shot the accused a piercing glare. Jun made an about turn and skulked off in a huff to lean against Taroo's car. Everyone beamed at Kenji, grateful that someone had finally stood up to pompous Jun.

Finally, light seeped through the blanket of darkness and morning dawned. There was no spectacular sunrise; in fact there was no sun at all – just light breaking through gloomy, steel grey clouds.

Dismayed, everyone returned to the cars moaning and complaining. They were all tired and damp. It felt like they'd all expected to see a terrific movie at the cinema to Takashi, only to walk out having watched a B-grade flop. He turned to see where the others were and he noticed Jun pass Akiko his business card before he came over towards Taroo's BMW. He looked very pleased with himself. Again it struck Takashi that Jun was a player. He glanced over at Haruka, but she hadn't noticed that exchange between Jun and Akiko, as she wasn't facing Taroo's car, and she'd been busy chatting with Momo-chan. *Surely I'm a better match for her than Jun,* Takashi thought to himself for the hundredth time since he'd met this insidious fellow.

'Sorry, everyone,' cried out Masaya. 'I was here two years ago and it was one of the most amazing experiences to see the sun rise from this point on the peninsula.'

'You're not to blame, Masaya,' Takashi said kindly.

Masaya shook his head. 'Still, it was my idea.'

'Let's go home, I'm exhausted,' said Yuriko's brother Taroo.

Hopping into the car, Takashi felt his spirits lift a little when Yuriko offered Jun the front seat. He felt a little childish knowing that Jun was no longer sitting right next to Haruka, but it wasn't long before there was another turn for the worse.

They were circling down the mountain, driving at a safe speed on a steep incline. Takashi felt extremely tired, but he couldn't sleep. Suddenly, the tyres hit the gravel and the head of the car began moving towards the side of the cliff. The drop below was at least a hundred metres. Yuriko screamed at her brother Taroo and he swerved back on to the road.

'You're an idiot! Turn on the radio and stay awake, or you'll kill us all,' she barked at him.

Takashi looked out the car window and watched the rain stream down the glass like falling tears. He said nothing, but now he was fuming inside. He felt his face flush up so much that his cheeks were burning. It reminded him of when he used to have rosy cheeks almost permanently as a child. He must have been about eight years old when his older brother – the brother for whom his family still mourned – used to joke that his cheeks were sometimes so red that he looked like he'd finished off a whole bottle of whisky. Takashi missed him a lot just then.

Breaking from his thoughts, Takashi noticed that no one was in the mood for conversation. Everybody kept quiet for the remainder of the journey back to Tokyo.

Takashi finally staggered back into his apartment at about noon. He flung off his shoes at the door and dialled his parents' number. Thankfully, his mother answered the phone with her usual cheerful voice.

'It's me,' Takashi said. 'I'm furious.'

'Happy New Year, Takashi,' his mother said. She made him feel bad for not acknowledging the day. He already felt really guilty for not being there to celebrate with them, but it would've been too difficult to get to their house and meet up with them that day. Anyway, his mother was always busy at New Year cleaning the entire house and he would have been in the way, he thought to himself. On New Year's Eve, his parents would have watched the NHK broadcast of the music programme *Kōhaku Uta Gassen* and today they'd probably have visited a shrine to commemorate the first day of the year.

'Sorry, Happy New Year,' said Takashi.

'What's the matter? Has something terrible happened?' she said.

'I went to the Izu peninsula with Masaya and Kenji and a few others and Haruka was there. She practically ignored me and spent all her time with a guy called Jun who is probably the most annoying person I've ever met.'

'Haruka is a nice girl,' said his mother in a soothing voice. 'I don't think she'd be interested in spending much time with this person if he really is so horrible.'

'Well she looked pretty interested in him to me,' replied Takashi. He went on to explain to her how they were nearly all killed in an accident. His mother listened without interruption until he paused to catch his breath.

'My dear Takashi,' his mother said to him calmly and softly. 'I'm sure that Yuriko's brother Taroo didn't mean to endanger your lives. Please try and look at it from another perspective. He did go to a lot of trouble to drive you all the way to Izu. It is a long drive.'

'So what?' said Takashi. 'He shouldn't drive if he can't keep his eyes on the road. Can I speak to Father?' he asked.

'He's sleeping.'

'I should sleep, too. I'll speak to you later,' said Takashi.

'Just keep working hard at your studies, Takashi. That should be your priority.'

'Of course,' Takashi replied.

He put the phone down and thought about what his mother had said. She did have a point. He decided he needed a better perspective on life, just as she'd suggested.

Takashi needed to get to sleep, but his mind was restless. He wanted to call Haruka, but he didn't know if she was interested in talking to him. He decided to send her a text message: "Do you still want to meet in Omotesando next Thursday?"

She sent him back a message immediately: "The café is probably closed for New Year. I can meet you there in two weeks."

"Terrific. I'll be there at 6:30 p.m.," Takashi replied. He felt a lot better, and he went to sleep for a very long time.

CHAPTER 15

The good will is in all

It was eight thirty p.m. on Wednesday, the second week in January. Haruka had been wandering through Omotesando that evening after work, looking through the shops, wishing she didn't need to be so careful with her money now. As she passed by the Café hors et dans, she imagined Takashi sitting there waiting for her the next day, and she wished that it were Thursday. Her heart was still torn between Takashi and Jun. She wanted to hold onto Takashi for her sake, yet she knew that being with Jun would make her parents happy and provide financial stability for her in the future.

When she was with Jun, she would often think about Takashi. She'd remember how he could make her laugh and how much she looked forward to his phone calls – even talking about the weather with Takashi would make her smile. She sometimes had to cancel her dates with him on a Thursday, but it upset her when she did. Despite this, it wasn't always perfect. Occasionally when she met with Takashi at the café in Omotesando, he'd talk about the cost of this or that and it was then she'd realise that if they had money problems in the future, this might pull them apart. On the train ride home, Haruka kept asking herself why love had to be so difficult.

A couple of hours later, as soon as Haruka opened the front door, she knew that something was going on. There was a commotion inside. Her father rushed past quickly holding three pairs of socks. Her mother called out to her in an agitated voice from the bedroom.

'Where've you been, Haruka? Well, don't bother telling me. You've probably been out with that Takashi fellow. You're wasting your time with him,' she said. 'I need to have a quick talk with you. Please come in and sit down so we can have a chat.'

'I don't meet Takashi on Wednesdays,' Haruka said to her. 'I was window shopping after work.' She entered her parents' bedroom and sat down on the edge of the bed, a little confused.

'We've been waiting for quite some time for Jun to propose, haven't we, Haruka?' her mother said to her.

'Yes, but I'm quite sure that he's waiting until I move to Kyoto,' Haruka replied defensively. She wasn't expecting her mother to broach this subject as soon as she walked in the door.

'I've spoken to your father and we think that you and Jun are floundering, so we've decided that we should go to Kyoto and meet with his parents again to start arranging wedding plans with him and his family.'

'If you think that's best,' Haruka replied, knowing that this would make her mother happy.

'Yes, we do, Haruka. You'd better hurry up and pack, my dear, because I have a surprise for you – we're going to Kyoto in the morning and you must get ready and join us. Now go and get a move on.'

Haruka wanted more than anything to make her parents happy. The thought of a big, expensive wedding, living in a lovely house and buying everything that her heart desired, which would all be possible if she married Jun, now made perfect sense to her. Haruka's mother gave her a knowing smile as she turned to continue with her packing, but it suddenly occurred to Haruka that she might not be able to go at all.

'But Mother, I have to work tomorrow, so I can't go with you,' she said despondently.

'I've spoken to your work. They were very nice about it, and they've given you the time off.'

'You've spoken to my work?' Haruka asked her mother, grinning from one ear to the other. Normally Haruka wouldn't be happy about her mother speaking to her boss without talking to her first, but that evening, she secretly thanked her mother with all her heart.

'Yes, dear,' she replied. 'I spoke to your work a few hours ago and they said that would be fine. They even suggested you call in to see Mrs Aoki at the English conversation school to finalise any details about your new management position.'

'That's terrific,' said Haruka. 'I really want to ask if they've organised my accommodation.'

'I spoke to Yuriko's mother this morning, and she said she needs to go to Kyoto to visit a sick friend, and I thought to myself that this was the perfect opportunity for us to meet up with her sister, Jun's mother, don't you think?'

'Yes, of course, Mother,' Haruka said with a laugh. She gave her mother a fun salute as she skipped out of the room to start her own packing.

Haruka was in her room, half packed, trying to decide which of her silk scarves to take with her when it dawned on her that she should contact Takashi because she wouldn't be able to meet him in Tokyo the following evening. Haruka tried to call him several times, but she couldn't get through. Panicking, she called Yuriko's home, hoping that her friend could offer her some advice on what to do, but Yuriko's phone went to voicemail as well. Haruka decided that the best thing to do would be to go and see her next door. She'd have plenty of time to finish her packing later.

—⁓—

When Haruka rang the doorbell at Yuriko's house, her mother, Mrs Makimoto, opened their front door.

'Hello Haruka,' she said. 'Are you coming along with your parents to Kyoto?'

Haruka wasn't sure if Mrs Makimoto was willing to discuss with her their plans to meet up with Jun and his family to talk about the wedding, so she didn't mention anything to her about this.

'I certainly am,' Haruka replied. 'I'm sorry it's late, but I really need to see Yuriko. Is she in her room?'

'I'm not sure,' Mrs Makimoto said. 'Go up and take a look.' She walked away with no intention of continuing the conversation. Haruka was used to her frosty demeanour, so it didn't bother her in the slightest.

At the top of the stairs, Haruka crossed the landing and knocked on Yuriko's door. She opened it and gave her a generous smile as she beckoned Haruka into her room. Haruka was so pleased to see that Yuriko's bedroom had been totally transformed. She looked around in astonishment. The pink walls and fluffy toys had been replaced by a tasteful, sophisticated and glamorous boudoir, and the exercise bike was nowhere to be seen.

A padded satin cream headboard offset a luxurious off-white bed cover with organza pleats and a pearl trim. Haruka was also pleased to see a novel by Yukio Mishima instead of Yuriko's diet magazines on top of one of her new ivory bedside tables that had lovely butterfly drop handles. The candy-striped sofa seat had also disappeared and in its place was an 18th century style lady's chair. On the floor was freshly laid thick pile carpet in a soft mocha colour. In the corner was a cream dressing table with a Bordeaux mirror, accompanied by a matching upholstered stool with stylish tapered feet. The walls had been covered in beige wallpaper that was embossed with an elegant, pearly wisteria pattern.

'What do you think?' said Yuriko as she extended her right arm outwards to display the room.

'Unbelievable!' Haruka replied. She was so pleased to see that Yuriko had also taken heed of her makeup advice and kept it light and natural looking. Her skin had greatly improved, and she looked very pretty. Her high cheekbones were now emphasized and her eyes sparkled without heavy eye shadow.

'The room is completely transformed – it looks so beautiful. It's so elegant and grown up,' said Haruka as she felt the organza bedding and admired her new dressing table.

'I know,' replied Yuriko. 'I spoke to my father a couple of weeks ago and he had the decorators in on Monday. I'm so happy, I don't want to leave the room!'

'I wouldn't either, if I had a bedroom like this,' Haruka said wriggling her toes in the thick pile of the carpet.

'And I have some exciting news to share with you,' said Yuriko, sinking into the lovely new lady's chair.

'Tell me,' Haruka said.

'I went for an interview yesterday and I start a new part-time job next week.'

'How exciting,' said Haruka, really pleased that Yuriko's life was going so well for her lately and she had more to think about than just dieting and shopping.

'You know I did a three-month interior design course at the end of last year.'

'Yes,' Haruka replied. 'You thought that course was really interesting, didn't you?'

'Yes, I did,' said Yuriko. 'Well, I saw a job advertised a couple of weeks ago. They needed someone to work with an interior designer in Shinagawa two days a week, and I went to the interview last Friday. It went really well, and I found out today that I'll be starting in two weeks.'

'That's great news, I'm really happy for you,' Haruka said to her, delighted she'd finally found a job she wanted to do.

So I thought I'd better go shopping and buy myself a whole lot of stylish winter clothes for my new job.' Yuriko said as she walked over to her built-in wardrobes and slid back the door. She pulled out the most luxurious pair of black tailored trousers, a short, fitted silver grey cashmere jacket and several silk blouses. Haruka's eyes opened wide with admiration. The price tags were still on each garment, but she could not see one brand name slashed across the front. They were really beautiful subtle pieces of the finest quality.

'You're a lucky girl, Yuriko,' she said. 'They're all really beautiful– but what's that big bag at the bottom of your wardrobe?'

'That's my surprise for you,' Yuriko replied. 'In that bag are the clothes I've never worn because they're a size too big. I thought you might like them – they're all brand new.'

Haruka sensed an opportunity. She'd cut back her shopping budget to zero and now, thanks to Yuriko, she'd have a new set of clothes and she wouldn't have to dent her credit card. Haruka opened up the bag and rummaged through the garments that were all folded neatly ready for her inspection. She was delighted – six out of the eight pieces would be perfect. She'd just gained two Ralph Lauren striped tops, a long cream belted coat from Junko Shimada, two pairs of trousers from Comme des Garçons and a skirt from Issey Miyake's Pleats Please collection.

Haruka shook her head in amazement. 'Are you sure you don't want these, Yuriko?'

Yuriko was so happy to see that Haruka was so grateful. 'No, definitely not. You're my best friend. I want you to have them.'

'Thanks, Yuriko, you're the best,' said Haruka. 'By the way, are you coming to Kyoto? Are you packed?' she asked, suddenly remembering to ask Yuriko about the trip the next day. She was so astonished by the bedroom transformation, the news about the interior design job and the lovely new clothes she'd acquired that she'd almost forgotten the purpose of her visit.

'No, I'm not going. I have to look after my younger brother. He's only twelve, you know.'

'Oh, that's a pity, but....' Haruka started to say.

'What's the matter?' Yuriko asked her.

'Well, I have a problem and now that you're not going to Kyoto, maybe you could help me with a solution.'

'What's up?' she asked Haruka.

'I wanted to meet Takashi tomorrow in Omotesando, but I can't now. I called him to cancel our plans, but his phone is switched off and I can't get through to him. I think it would be rude to just leave another message, because I've had to cancel our dates quite a bit lately.'

'Where were you planning to meet?' asked Yuriko.

'At the usual place. Do you know the Café hors et dans in Omotesando, near the subway station?'

'Yes, I've been there several times before. It's above Morgan de toi, isn't it?'

'Yes, very good, Yuriko.'

'What time were you planning to meet?'

'Six thirty p.m.,' Haruka replied.

'No problem – I've been meaning to go to the Prada shop just near there for some time. I'll meet up with him and let him know that you're in Kyoto.'

'What about your little brother? You can't leave him,' said Haruka.

'I'll take him to cram school. He can study there for a few hours.'

'Thanks. You're an angel, Yuriko.'

'My pleasure,' she replied.

'Yuriko....'

'Yes?' she said.

'Just one thing – don't mention to Takashi that I'm meeting Jun in Kyoto,' Haruka said to her.

'He'll probably be able to work that one out, Haruka.'

'Oh yes ...well, try not to bring him up in the conversation,' Haruka said.

'I'll do my best. Have a good time in Kyoto.'

'Yuriko?'

'Yes, Haruka?'

'We're going to discuss wedding plans with Jun's family.'

'Good luck with that,' Yuriko replied, smiling fondly at her best friend.

They said their goodbyes and Haruka went back to her house next door to finish her packing, proudly holding her bag of new clothes. She was full of excitement about her trip to Kyoto.

CHAPTER 16

Evil gotten goods never prove well

They boarded the ten fifty-three Hikari Super Express Bullet Train from platform four at Shin-Yokohama station the following morning. Haruka and her parents, as well as Mrs Makimoto, Yuriko's mother, all settled into the comfortable brown velour seats for the two and a half hour trip to Kyoto. Haruka's father was restless for most of the journey. He ordered several snacks from the trolley lady and he made four or five trips to the smoking carriage, where he could sit and enjoy a cigarette. Haruka tried to call Takashi four times on the way, but his mobile was still turned off. The train travelled at about 270 kilometres per hour. They stopped at Odawara, Nagoya, Gifu-Hashima and Maibara before they finally pulled into Kyoto station.

Once they'd exited the station at Kyoto, a taxi escorted them to the Okura Hotel. They checked in at the grand reception and made their way to their rooms on the seventh floor. Haruka's parents had kindly paid for her to have a room of her own.

Opening the door to a spacious suite, Haruka was so happy to be in Kyoto. Her room was beautifully decorated and the bed looked so comfortable and enticing with its fluffy pillows cradling two elegant paper cranes, sitting above smooth and fresh-looking sateen sheets. She was almost tempted to take a quick nap, but Haruka thought she'd better call the English conversation school and ask about the accommodation which they were organising for her.

Haruka dialled their number and asked to be put through to Mrs Aoki. After about thirty seconds she came to the phone and seemed very keen to speak to her.

'Hello Haruka,' she said. 'I'm really glad you called. I've just spoken to your manager in Harajuku and she told me you're in Kyoto. I have some news for you. Ordinarily, I'd ask you to come in and see me, but today I'm particularly busy, so I'm sorry, but I'm going to have to tell you this over the phone.'

'I don't understand,' Haruka said to her. 'Is there a problem?'

'I'm afraid there is,' she said. 'The woman whose job you were replacing is no longer joining her boyfriend in the US and has decided to retain her management position here in Kyoto.'

'I see,' Haruka said. 'So the position is no longer available?'

'Yes, that's right,' said Mrs Aoki. 'You were very well-qualified, and I'm sure you'll have no problem acquiring another management position elsewhere.'

'Thank you,' said Haruka, lost for words.

'I sincerely apologise for any inconvenience we may have caused you, Haruka,' were Mrs Aoki's final words.

Haruka put down the phone, sat on the end of the bed and hugged her knees into her chest. She'd really been looking forward to starting this new management position, and in just a few minutes, it had all been taken away from her. She'd done quite a bit of preparation for her new role, and she'd never expected this disappointment. Haruka had also been thinking about how she could get to know Jun's family a bit better before the wedding if she lived near them in Kyoto, but now she realised she wouldn't have that opportunity.

The telephone in the room rang and pulled Haruka out of her reverie. She picked up the receiver only to be told by her mother to join her and her father in their room down the hall. She changed into a skirt and went to join her parents.

If Haruka thought her room was lovely, theirs was a sight to behold. Two huge floor-to-ceiling windows afforded a marvellous view over the town of Kyoto, and in the distance one could see a postcard-like image of the Higashiyama mountain range.

Haruka's father had already helped himself to the mini-bar and was sitting on a love seat that was expensively draped in a soft floral mint fabric. He was enjoying a glass of 10-year-old Suntory Pure Malt Whisky.

'It's a little early for a drink, isn't it, Father?' Haruka teased him light-heartedly.

'Don't you start, Haruka,' he replied gruffly.

'I have some news to tell you,' she said to her parents. 'I've just spoken to the manager at the English conversation school here in Kyoto and I won't be working there because the position is no longer available.'

'Not to worry,' said her mother, who looked perfectly fine with that arrangement. 'Once you marry Jun, you won't be working anyway – you'll be too busy at home.'

'Maybe you're right,' Haruka replied.

'You can't sit around drinking all day,' her mother pointed out to her father as she padded around the room in the hotel slippers, trying to unpack a few clothes. 'We have to meet Mrs Makimoto in the lobby in fifteen minutes. Now, I can't find a handkerchief anywhere. I'm sure that I packed two or three. Don't tell me I left them on the bedside table before we left.'

'I have a spare one in my suitcase,' Haruka offered.

'Thank you, Haruka. Could you fetch it for me and meet us down in the lobby?' her mother asked her. She twirled around and looked at her husband. 'Please don't have another drink. We don't have time.'

Haruka could hear her father pouring himself a second glass as she left the room.

—ⅶ—

Haruka was waiting with Mrs Makimoto for about ten minutes before her mother and father joined them in the lobby. She discreetly passed her mother a Céline handkerchief that she slipped into her handbag.

'Will you meet up with us at six p.m. for dinner?' her mother asked Mrs Makimoto, who was about to go and see her sick friend.

'Yes,' she replied. 'Are you going to the Temple of the Golden Pavilion this afternoon?'

'Yes. And will Mrs Kurokawa and her son Jun be joining us tomorrow when we visit the Ryōan-ji Temple?' asked Haruka's mother sharing a smile with her daughter.

Haruka knew that she was clearly using this trip to bring Jun and her closer together as well as their two families.

'Oh yes,' Mrs Makimoto replied with confidence. 'They'll meet us after breakfast tomorrow at ten thirty a.m.'

Haruka's mother looked at her daughter again with a hugely satisfied smirk pasted across her face.

On the way to the Temple of the Golden Pavilion, Haruka and her parents were in a fine mood. They chatted all the way in high spirits, looking forward to the temple and really enjoying each other's company. Haruka had visited the Golden Temple with her junior high school, but its sheer brilliance still stunned her again that afternoon. The gold leaf that encompassed the temple and its reflection in the surrounding Kyôko-chi pond provided a serenity and splendour that created a real Zen sense of peacefulness.

Haruka's father took a photo of his wife and daughter with the Golden Temple in the background.

'The temple's exquisite, isn't it, Mother?' Haruka said.

'Yes, but it's the gardens that I like the most. Each branch and each rock are so beautifully sculptured. This is art for me, Haruka – the epitome of Japanese art,' her mother replied.

On the way back to the hotel, Haruka thought about her relationship with her mother. When she was growing up, they'd always been close, but she somehow felt that their trip to Kyoto and the visit to The Golden Temple had brought them even closer. Haruka was so grateful that her parents had decided to take this trip to Kyoto, even though they had money problems. It would all be worth it when they met up with Jun and his family and the wedding plans were arranged. Haruka thought that her mother obviously had her best interests at heart and if everything worked out with Jun, then she was looking forward to the harmony between their two families.

That night, Mrs Makimoto, Haruka and her family enjoyed a delicious dinner in the hotel's restaurant. Haruka returned to her room about ten p.m. and slept well, looking forward to the following day.

On Friday morning, she dressed with a little more care than usual, as she had the double pleasure of looking forward to seeing Jun again and more sightseeing and she wanted to look her best. Haruka remembered to wear the Tiffany & Co. heart pendant and the Hermés scarf that Jun had so generously given to her in August. She even took her Louis Vuitton bag with her that she only brought out for special occasions. When she'd finished dressing, Haruka went to her parents' room to find her father enjoying a delicious Japanese breakfast. It had obviously been brought to the room moments earlier. Her father looked up and suggested that Haruka order something herself while there was still time.

Haruka looked at the room service menu and also at the array of food in front of her father. He was holding his chopsticks over an appetiser, grilled fish, miso soup, and dried seaweed, vegetables simmering in sweet soy sauce, as well as egg, pickles, rice and fruit. Haruka didn't think she could stomach that much so early because she usually didn't eat breakfast. She ordered a grapefruit juice and a croissant, as well as a Danish pastry for her mother, and the food arrived shortly after.

Just after ten thirty a.m., they walked out of the elevator and into the spacious lobby to find Jun Kurokawa sitting with his mother. Mrs Kurokawa always made Haruka a bit nervous. A single band of grey hair running from the part at her hairline over her blackened perm made her look striking but quite intimidating.

Haruka was surprised to see Jun looking completely stupefied when he saw her and her parents. He stood up and offered them a crooked smile, visibly shaken by their appearance in the lobby.

'I didn't know that you were coming with my auntie to Kyoto,' were his first words.

'Didn't I mention it to you, Jun?' said his mother, waving to Mrs Makimoto as she walked across the lobby to join them.

'No, you didn't,' replied Jun.

'Hello Mr and Mrs Yoshino, how nice to see you both again. If there's anything I can do for you while you're in Kyoto, please let me know,' said Mrs Kurokawa to Haruka's parents.

Haruka had forgotten that Jun's mother had a superior and haughty voice. As she spoke to them, she looked upon Haruka and her parents with suspicion. Haruka's mother, who was usually very perceptive, seemed to be completely unaware of her tone and manner. Haruka thought that it was a little embarrassing to watch her mother trying to ingratiate herself with Mrs Kurokawa.

As they left the hotel, Jun's mother turned to Haruka, looking her up and down from head to toe.

'Really, young lady, your Hermés scarf and your Louis Vuitton handbag are lovely, but that's not an appropriate colour to be wearing at this time of the year. Who wears a long cream coat in this weather? Anyone can see that they're only going to get filthy. Maybe you and your mother could shop for something nicer now you're in Kyoto,' Mrs Kurokawa said to her imperiously.

Haruka looked down at her soft brown suede leather boots, co-ordinated with her beige jeans and the new Junko Shimada long cream belted coat that Yuriko had given her. Mrs Kurokawa was dressed entirely in black silk, angora and cashmere, and Haruka wanted to tell her that she looked like she was about to attend a funeral. Instead, she forced out the sweetest smile that she could manage. She wondered why she was receiving this treatment from her future mother-in-law.

'Shall we go to the Ryōan-ji Temple now? I'd have driven you myself, but the Mercedes is being serviced,' Mrs Kurokawa announced.

The pretentious tone in her voice did concern Haruka a little, but she told herself that when we they all got to know each other a little better, she would see a warmer and kinder side to her personality.

The stop for the bus to the Ryōan-ji Temple was opposite the Okura Hotel, and it wasn't long before their bus arrived. Jun stood beside Haruka on the way to the temple, but in the bus he said very little. Haruka was surprised by his lack of affection.

'You're looking well, Haruka. I've missed you,' Jun finally whispered to her.

'Why are you whispering, Jun?' Haruka asked, becoming more and more confused by his behaviour.

'I have a sore throat. I think I've caught a cold. Don't get too close to me, or you might catch it.'

'You poor thing,' Haruka replied. 'I hope you feel a bit better as the day goes on.'

Maybe I have nothing to worry about. Jun was probably acting strangely because he wasn't feeling very well, Haruka thought to herself.

'You know, Haruka, I think you should change your hairstyle,' Jun said to her, a little louder this time. 'Your hair would look so much better if you dyed it a lighter colour.'

'Do you think so?' Haruka replied, not sure whether he was paying her a compliment or being critical. She reassured herself that his suggestions and the way he teased her so often were due to the growing closeness between them and not because he was being unkind again.

'I do like my hair this colour,' she continued.

'Ultimately, it's your choice, but I must still insist that it would look better lighter. I know a great hairdresser in Kyoto who could do it for you,' said Jun.

'I'll think about it,' Haruka replied.

She noticed that her mother had been watching them and she gave her a look as if to ask what was wrong.

Haruka just dropped her head and looked at her feet. Jun looked out the window and said nothing for the rest of the bus trip.

'Look, here's our stop. Come on, let's get off the bus,' Haruka said to Jun. He held back to wait for his mother and Haruka stepped off the bus with her parents. She was a little taken aback by Jun's unfriendliness.

At the remarkable rock garden of the Ryōan-ji Temple, renowned for its quintessential portrayal of Zen art, Haruka found another good reason to be grateful for joining her parents on this trip. The sightseeing was so lovely for them to share as a family. It was the first time she had seen the fifteen rocks resting in a sea of perfectly swept light grey gravel and like the many other visitors who looked at this 15th century masterpiece, Haruka was overwhelmed by its sense of calm and happiness. She imagined the large rocks representing the mountains and the moss surrounding them to be the land that stretched from the foot of the hills to the sea. To her, the gravel represented the ocean that swept in waves around the land and undulated peacefully until it met another stretch of land or another world. She wondered if all those sitting around her had entirely different interpretations of this formidable piece of landscape art.

Everyone felt spiritually enriched as they silently gazed over the garden and after reading the inscription on the stone washed basin in the tearoom – "I learn only to be contented" – they felt that they came away with a better appreciation of the Zen philosophy.

Unfortunately, discontent was not far away upon their return to the hotel. In the lobby, Haruka and her mother were talking to Jun's mother Mrs Kurokawa about visiting Nijo Castle the following day, and Haruka's mother offered Mrs Kurokawa their home phone number in Ōfune. She watched her mother searching for a pen to write down the number, but Mrs Kurokawa was quicker to take out a pen of her own. It looked like her father's missing black and silver Mont Blanc pen – it even had the same scratch on the lid!

Haruka and her mother looked at the pen and then back at each other. Their mouths were wide open with disbelief. Haruka realised her mother recognised the pen that Haruka's father had supposedly misplaced during Jun's visit to their home in Ōfune months ago.

'What a … what a … beautiful pen,' Haruka's mother stuttered, trying to regain her composure. The vein in her forehead was throbbing.

'Oh yes, it is,' replied Mrs Kurokawa. 'Junichiro gave it to me for my birthday last week. Unfortunately, he scratched the lid when he was wrapping it.'

'Jun gave it to you for your birthday,' cried Haruka's mother in despair, her face now the colour of rice paper. 'How nice of him,' she managed to say.

Haruka could see by the look on her face that she wanted to snatch back the pen that rightfully belonged to them, but her mother was much too polite to do that.

'Yes, Mrs Yoshino,' replied Mrs Kurokawa. Why she continued to spit out their surname whenever she pronounced it, Haruka did not know. 'He's a wonderful son, and I will soon have a terrific daughter-in-law,' Mrs Kurokawa continued. 'He's just asked a gorgeous girl called Sakurako to marry him. Her father is the general manager of a huge textile company. They'll make a lovely couple and her family will obviously be an excellent business connection.'

Haruka and her mother were absolutely flabbergasted. They couldn't believe what Mrs Kurokawa had just said. Haruka noticed huge tears beginning to well up in her mother's eyes.

'Is that right?' her mother exclaimed, patting her face with her handkerchief.

Turning, Mrs Kurokawa looked at Haruka with great pity etched across her face and said in a snobbish voice, 'I hope that you find a nice husband. You're not getting any younger, are you, Haruka? Maybe a factory worker or someone that has a Pachinko gambling business … that would suit you very well wouldn't it?' Looking back at Haruka's mother, she continued, 'Mrs Yoshino, your husband looks like he enjoys a bit of Pachinko gambling. Am I right?'

Luckily, Haruka's mother refused to lower herself to Mrs Kurokawa's level by responding with a catty remark. She just shook her head in disbelief. If Mrs Kurokawa had wanted to humiliate and degrade them, she'd certainly achieved that, but Haruka's mother was not the type to be rude, especially to a lady that they'd only met a couple of times.

Jun walked over to join them, oblivious to what had just happened and to the words that had burst forth from his mother's cruel mouth.

'How about dinner tonight, Haruka?' he asked with an annoying confidence.

Haruka looked at him blankly and nodded towards his mother holding the Mont Blanc pen. He saw the pen, made the connection, and realising he'd been discovered as a thief, turned to hurry away, making some excuse about dropping his keys earlier or something to that effect. Haruka strode up to him and reached his side as he paused at the flower arrangement in the centre of the lobby.

'I need to talk to you, Jun. Your mother just told us that you're planning to marry a girl called Sakurako. So why have you been taking me out, continuously complimenting me and leading me and my mother to believe that you were going to ask me to marry you?' she demanded to know.

'Marry you? When did I ever mention marriage to you?' he replied. He looked down at Haruka, quite amused at her presumption that he was going to propose to her.

'Well … um….' Haruka was trying to think fast, but she was too furious to think logically. 'Um … Yuriko saw the engagement ring you bought in Ginza and we've just thought for quite a while now that … um….'

'And you thought the ring was for you, did you?' said Jun, laughing at Haruka's mistake.

'Of course I did,' she replied. 'Well, we were dating quite seriously … you even took me out for kaiseki-ryōri in Ginza. You don't take friends to a restaurant that expensive unless you're dating. You had Yuriko, my mother and I all convinced that you were my boyfriend, and we all thought it was serious.' Haruka pulled out the Tiffany & Co. heart pendant from under her scarf. 'And what about this romantic gift you bought me?'

'I didn't actually buy those,' he replied.

'Did you steal them?' she asked him.

'No … the pendants I gave you and your mother belonged to my sister and she never actually wore them, so she said I could take them and give them to you as presents – and since they were still in their original boxes....'

'And the scarves?' said Haruka, pointing to her Hermés scarf.

'I bought those,' he replied. 'Listen, Haruka, I have to tell you that I get bored, and that's the reason I took you out a few times,' Jun said to her, more gently this time as he watched tears fall down her cheeks. 'I think you're nice and very pretty, but it was never going to be serious.'

'Well you could have mentioned Sakurako,' Haruka hissed back at him, spitting out each word. She turned away from him and stormed back to her parents' side, wishing she'd never met Jun.

Haruka's mother had taken out the handkerchief again that she'd handed to her that morning and was dabbing her cheeks as she stood with her father away from the others. Haruka went up to her and put her hand on her shoulder.

'Haruka, I think a bug has flown into my eye – could you have a look at it in the bathroom with me, please?' she said to her. They turned adroitly and made for the ladies room, arm in arm – mortified and humiliated by this turn of events.

In the bathroom, Haruka's mother let her tears flow naturally. Haruka didn't shed any more tears, as she was now more angry than upset. As she held her mother's shoulders, it occurred to her that she was more concerned about the Kurokawa family upsetting her mother than her questionable relationship with Jun. *Damn that family*, she thought to herself.

'I'm sorry, Haruka,' her mother said to her. 'I should never have organised this trip to Kyoto.'

'It's not your fault, it's mine,' Haruka replied. 'When Yuriko told me about the engagement ring, I should have realised it wasn't for me.'

'No, Haruka,' said her mother firmly. 'It's all Jun's fault. He encouraged both you and me to believe he was really interested in you again. He even invited us to Kyoto. Do you remember that all those months ago when you came back from your date with Takashi?'

'Yes,' Haruka replied. She was now thinking of Takashi and how wonderful he'd been through this whole ordeal.

'I think you should call Takashi as soon as we get back to Ōfune,' said her mother, as though she was reading her daughter's mind.

They left the ladies' room and Haruka and her mother joined her father at the elevator.

'We'll meet at seven p.m. for dinner, Haruka,' her mother said with the voice of a mouse as they made their way to the seventh floor.

Haruka noticed her father comforting her mother as they walked to their room.

'With all the nice people in Kyoto, why did we have to meet up again with the Kurokawas?' Haruka's mother said to her father.

'You did have a lovely time at the Ryōan-ji Temple though, didn't you?' he said to her.

Mrs Makimoto, Haruka and her parents all dined in the Gion district that evening. Haruka thought that it was nice to have a break from Jun and his mother. After dinner, the sight of a Maiko apprentice geisha amused Haruka's father. They stopped to watch her from a distance. She was dressed in a blue silk kimono. Delicate flowers fell from her ornate hairstyle at her collar. The nape of her neck was provocatively exposed. She briefly turned in their direction before stepping into a waiting taxi, giving them a faint glimpse of her ethereal floating world.

The next day, Haruka was pleased to hear that Jun would not be joining them for their last morning in Kyoto.

She was so proud of her mother, who walked with her head high, keeping her distance from Mrs Kurokawa as they wandered through Nijo Castle, the official residence of the first Tokugawa Shogun, Ieyasu. Haruka stood by her side and took many charming photos of her mother and her father together. They posed in front of the surrounding gardens and the stonework that beautifully complemented this splendid building. Haruka learnt from her father that it had been built in the early Edo period of the 17th century.

The whole morning, Mrs Kurokawa stayed by her sister's side, whispering and laughing in the most annoying way.

Later, after returning to the hotel, Haruka tried to call Takashi in Tokyo on her mobile. Again, he did not answer. She even tried calling him from the hotel's landline, but to no avail. His mobile was off, and she could only hope that Yuriko had managed to meet up with him and that Jun's name had not been mentioned.

Their train bound for Tokyo was leaving at two o'clock. They arrived at the station in good time at one fifteen p.m. Haruka excused herself as they entered the waiting room and made her way to the ladies' toilet.

Pushing open the door of the ladies' room, she noticed all the cubicles were vacant. She rushed into the toilet on the far end, pulling three or four tissues from her Louis Vuitton handbag, and sat sobbing uncontrollably. Haruka allowed all the hurt, embarrassment and anger to gush out of her, and she kept this up for a solid five minutes. She was upset about losing her job in Kyoto and about Jun's lies and the way he used her because he was so "bored" with his life, but most of all she was upset for her parents who'd wasted a lot of money coming to Kyoto, only to be completely humiliated and degraded by the Kurokawa family.

Finally, feeling a bit better after getting that out of her system, Haruka composed herself, flushed the toilet out of habit, and opened the door. A very well-dressed middle-aged woman in a fur hat that matched the fur collar on her camel cashmere coat had entered the ladies' room and her reflection in the mirror opposite bounced back at Haruka. She was frowning at Haruka's dishevelled face. Admittedly, Haruka knew she looked awful, even a bit spooky. Haruka managed a wonky smile back at her, straightened her shoulders and retrieved another tissue from her designer bag.

Wetting the corner of the tissue, Haruka wiped away the black mascara running down her strained face. She reapplied her lashes with her Lancôme mascara and brightened her lips with a Chanel lipstick. To finish, she brushed on lashings of her Touche Éclat highlighter to disguise the dark circles under her puffy eyes. Pleased with her mini makeover, Haruka forced out a bright smile and standing tall, she left the judgemental lady and made her way back to her parents, determined not to be emotional.

Yuriko's mother had decided to rush around buying small cakes and other souvenirs before they departed from Kyoto station. While Mrs Makimoto was deciding between red bean-paste cakes and green tea sweets, Haruka's mother asked her daughter various questions in the waiting room underneath the platforms about Takashi.

'How old is that boy Takashi now?' she asked.

'Twenty-one years old, Mother,' replied Haruka.

'And he's nearly finished at university, hasn't he?'

'Yes, Mother.'

'He's such an honest boy. No pretence. Just a really kind and honest person, isn't he, Haruka?'

'Yes,' she replied.

'I like his values, Haruka. He's not the type of boy who is always trying to impress his friends, is he?'

'No, Mother – he has a mind of his own.'

'You do get along really well, don't you? What are his parents like, Haruka?'

'Yes, we get along well. I only met his parents once when I was at university, but they're very nice.'

'Does he drink a lot?'

'No, Mother.'

'But he smokes?'

'Yes, but Father smokes as well, doesn't he?'

Haruka's mother looked lovingly at her husband and her voice softened, 'Takashi was always there for you when your father was ill, wasn't he? You must invite him over more often, Haruka.'

'Yes, Mother,' she replied. 'Although he's not really wealthy, he should get a good job after university.'

'Don't worry about that, Haruka,' said her mother. 'After this weekend, I've had just as much as I can take of wealthy, pretentious people. We'll manage somehow.'

Haruka sighed with relief. Although she was embarrassed that they'd all fallen so easily for Jun's pretentious ways, it was because of him she could see that Takashi's kindness was so much better for her than Jun's false charms. Her only worry was that it might be too late. She had to hope that Takashi still felt the same way about her. She thought that he may very well have dubious feelings towards her now that he'd learned that she'd been to Kyoto, even if Yuriko hadn't spoken one word about Jun.

Haruka sat restlessly on the bullet train on their way back to Shin-Yokohama. Her anxiety heightened with each station that they passed. Her greatest fear now was that Takashi would no longer take her seriously. She thought that it was so important for them to be together. He brought out the best in her. She thought that he was kind, honest, reliable and dependable and also very attractive. She decided that he surely had his own faults like everyone else, but faults that she could easily accept. The question she kept asking herself was whether he would be able to accept her faults. Haruka thought back to the romantic night at his apartment and the strong pang of jealousy she'd felt when he'd flirted with Akiko at Masaya's tavern. She knew at that moment that she'd be honoured to go out with a person like Takashi, who had so much to offer her.

CHAPTER 17

The nettle grows where the rose was expected

If Takashi thought the trip to Izu was an utter failure, the worst was yet to come.

Two weeks later, he was waiting as planned in Omotesando at the Café hors et dans. He was nervous, but he was looking forward to seeing Haruka. He wanted to speak to her about her relationship with Jun. He also wanted her to be more open about her feelings for him.

Maybe the cold had sent everyone else home that evening. Only two other people were at the café – a girl and an older man. It was painful to watch this couple, because the girl, wearing a pink top stretched over a rotund pregnant belly, had tears escaping down her cheeks. All Takashi could hear from her was the occasional sob. Sitting opposite her was a very stiff and hostile businessman in his thirties, refusing to speak to her or offer any consolation. Takashi turned away, not allowing himself to even begin to imagine what type of situation was unravelling over there.

The hands on Takashi's watch showed 6:50 p.m. Haruka had never been this late before, and for a minute his stomach turned. He thought that she'd forgotten about their plans to meet. Takashi lowered his head and stared blankly at the floor, thinking of the time that

Haruka had dropped her money there and had nearly lost ¥50,000.

At six fifty-five p.m., it was not Haruka who walked through the door. It was Yuriko.

Yuriko sat down with a forced smile on her face and Takashi panicked. She carefully placed several shopping bags down next to her.

'Where's Haruka? Is she ill?' he asked her.

'Haruka's fine,' Yuriko replied. 'She asked me to come and meet you here because she's in Kyoto. She tried to call you, but your mobile phone must've been out of range.'

Takashi was completely confused, upset and worried. Not a good combination. He felt like he was going to be sick.

'My mother wanted to go to Kyoto to see a sick friend and she didn't want to go on the bullet train alone. So Haruka's mother said that she'd accompany her and Haruka wanted to go along with them.'

'Why didn't you go to Kyoto?' Takashi asked her.

'I'm looking after my little brother while they're away,' she replied.

The waitress came over and, sensing that something was not right, but afraid that Yuriko might not order a drink, stood hovering behind them. Takashi nodded in the direction of the girl.

Yuriko turned and ordered a cake. 'I'll have a fruit tart, please.'

'And I'll have another coffee,' said Takashi. This struck him as odd, as he'd only ordered a coffee, yet Yuriko was actually planning to eat something. He thought that she must have been stressed, but she looked well enough.

'How long are they staying in Kyoto?' he asked Yuriko.

'Three days. They wanted to do some sightseeing and catch up with friends.'

'Will they be visiting Jun and his family?' Takashi asked.

'You might as well know the truth, Takashi. Haruka and her mother are going to Kyoto to discuss wedding plans with Jun's family,' Yuriko replied with hesitation.

Takashi felt like the wind had been knocked out of him. Determined not to show his shock and disappointment, he straightened his back and stared straight into Yuriko's eyes. 'Well, I thought Haruka and Jun were getting serious. Tell Haruka that I wish her all the very best and I won't bother her again as she's obviously in love with Jun and I refuse to interfere.'

'I'm so sorry, Takashi,' said Yuriko.

'There's nothing to be sorry about,' he replied.

'Surely you can still be friends,' she pleaded with him.

'No, we can't,' Takashi replied firmly.

The fruit tart and Takashi's coffee arrived and he sat gloomily looking into his drink. Yuriko, who was usually so loquacious, now sat there eating her cake trying not to drop any crumbs on her skirt. She was looking and acting differently today, but he couldn't figure out the reason for this. It wasn't just the fact that she was eating something. He thought her hair looked nice and her makeup looked more natural, but that wasn't it. He noticed her face was a little fuller, but that wasn't it either. Yuriko was more at ease with herself – that's what it was, he decided.

'You didn't come especially to Omotesando just to meet me, did you?' Takashi asked her.

'No – I wanted to do some shopping nearby, and so it wasn't a problem for me to come here.'

'Thanks,' he replied. Yuriko was telling the truth. Next to her on the seat were several shopping bags covered in designer labels. He looked at her with envy. Her family had so much money and she could have whatever she wanted.

Takashi finished his drink and gave Yuriko the excuse that he had a lot of study to complete. They said goodbye to each other at the door of the coffee shop. Takashi needed to be alone.

He walked to the station feeling like a bubble of anger was once again fermenting inside of him. He felt like a pressurised rice cooker that was letting out short bursts of steam from the lid.

This feeling inside him remained there over the next twenty-four hours. He left his mobile off so he couldn't take any calls. He channelled all this negative energy into studying for his upcoming exams. This was his driving force and surprisingly enough, he thought that he'd do better in his tests because of the way he felt inside.

Takashi barged through each hour like a bullet. The time passed by quickly, and his only direction now was to concentrate on his studies and his career. He felt that he'd been stupid to allow himself to get tangled up in feelings for a girl when his future was at stake.

Recently, Takashi had been sleeping all day and waking at nine at night. He would venture out into the dark to buy something to eat such as a ready meal from the convenience store. He'd eaten so many meals from there while he was studying that he'd now acquired a real taste for those bland microwave dinners. His favourite at the moment was a pack of two hamburgers in sauce at the wonderful price of just ¥398. Takashi knew he could live pretty well between his home and that store, and though he wasn't on friendly terms with the people that worked there, they certainly recognised him and gave him a friendly nod when he walked through their sliding doors.

He'd been sleeping so much lately that his mind was foggy when he woke up. If he'd finished his studying, he'd try to watch some late TV, but he wasn't able to follow the programmes properly. His mind was elsewhere, and he was getting more lethargic during the day. Sometimes Takashi could not help but think about Haruka. *Will I just become a fleeting friend on the road of life?* he'd often think to himself.

CHAPTER 18

One loss brings another

This New Year brought with it a slice of freezing temperatures that would continue for a couple of months. The cold wrapped its fingers around Takashi's heart and his bones.

Despite this icy weather, he continued to study hard and do what he felt was expected of him as he tried to force images of Haruka out of his mind. He'd been a good student at school and he really wanted to work for an elite company. He was determined to do well at university and he'd bury his head in his textbooks at home so that he could continue to prepare for the exams ahead. Each hour blended into the next, and as usual he was buried deep in his studies on the second Friday in January when the floor beneath him began to shudder and tremble.

He hoped that this earthquake would be as insignificant as those he'd experienced a few months before. But this one felt different. The room started to move in waves, indicating that it might be a lot worse. Time moved like a rubber band, expanding and constricting over and over.

Being a student, Takashi couldn't afford to live in the more modern apartments supported by rubber plates that moved the building with the tremors. His home didn't have anything that protected its foundations from major fractures, for it was about forty years old. He knew that if an earthquake was strong enough, he could end up buried under many layers of steel, brick and concrete. Since he was little, he'd always felt a comforting sense of relief when a bad earthquake had just passed. He'd often feel a renewed sense of gratitude for his health and his life. However, that didn't mean that he did not panic when they occurred.

With this thought in mind, Takashi quickly threw on some clothes, hoping that the earthquake would stop with one shake. Unfortunately for him, it didn't and when the room shook for the second and then the third time, he grabbed his wallet and his keys and threw on a jacket. He wasn't sure whether he should run outside or stay inside and hope for the best. He was less afraid about getting hurt and more concerned about losing all his belongings. The room rattled even more. Takashi dived under the coffee table and cushioned his head with a pillow, hoping the shaking and shuddering would stop.

The table shook. The light swayed violently back and forth. The room now seemed eerie. He gazed straight ahead. His knuckles went white as he clung to the leg of the coffee table. He told himself to keep breathing. It was in between the third and fourth tremor that the fear within him slowed down time. Now the room was moving like huge waves in a storm. His feet felt like they were already buried in rubble. He tried to move, but he couldn't. His eyes just focused on the glass of water sitting on the top of the television. He watched as the water swayed up one side and then the other. Finally the glass tipped onto the floor and liquid cascaded down the screen of the TV. This broke him from his reverie. At the same time, the tremors stopped and the spilt water was the only evidence that an earthquake had occurred.

Takashi knew that earthquakes like this could be followed by even bigger tremors, minutes or even hours later. He wasn't looking forward to a fearful night ahead. He never slept well after such big scares. Takashi slept in his clothes, and he kept the light on until morning. Though he woke up several times, half-expecting the walls to be falling down around him, there were no more disturbances.

The following morning, Takashi woke early after just a few hours' sleep to watch the news about the previous night's earthquake on the television. It was reported that the quake measured 6.2 on the Richter scale. Not powerful enough to devastate the city, but he learned that many were left injured. The reporter spoke in a grave tone about the inevitability of a more formidable earthquake that could destroy Tokyo and affect the thirty million people that lived in and around the city.

Japan is seismically active due to the fact that the county sits on top of a jigsaw of tectonic plates. Takashi had been trained since childhood on how to take action if and when an earthquake occurred. Unfortunately, no one could predict when or how destructive any future quakes would be. Each time they occurred, the people of Japan strove to learn from the experience and use that information to help them cope better in the future.

Takashi took a shower and quickly got ready to go out, determined to meet Masaya in Shibuya, despite the threat of another earthquake.

He'd just finished dressing when his mobile rang. He took the call even though he was hurrying to get ready. Takashi was surprised to hear his father's voice. He sounded terrible.

'I have some bad news, Takashi,' his father said. His voice was shaking.

Takashi presumed something terrible had happened to his parents during the earthquake, but his father had called to talk about his own mother, and the news was upsetting.

'Your grandmother passed away yesterday at her home,' he said to Takashi, who fell to the floor and felt like he'd been smacked across the face.

'That's shocking news,' Takashi said. His voice was shaky and he found it difficult to find the right words to say. 'This is sudden. I didn't even know she was ill.'

'Nor did we,' his father replied. 'Every week when I went to see her, she never mentioned a word about being sick.'

Takashi could hear how tired his father was, and he was shocked by his croaky voice, which was full of grief.

'I spoke to her doctor and he told me she'd been to see him a few weeks back. He'd discovered that she had an advanced form of throat cancer that had also spread to other parts of her body. He'd suggested she start treatment immediately, but he knew that no matter what he did, he wouldn't be able to help her,' said his father.

'That's awful,' said Takashi.

'When I saw her last week she had no colour in her cheeks and I asked her how she was and she said she was fine,' said his father. 'I thought she was so pale because the room was freezing and she hadn't turned the heating on.'

'Who called you to say that she'd passed away?' Takashi asked.

'Her neighbour and close friend, Mrs Ikeda, dropped in to see her at about lunch time and she was devastated to find her stone cold in her bed. She rang an ambulance and me straight away. We rushed over to her house and when we arrived, we were told that she must have died in her sleep. Her face was so serene and she looked so content,' sobbed his father.

'So she was really ill, but she just didn't want anyone to know?' Takashi asked him gently. 'She must have been in denial about her illness.'

'It looks that way. We did have a long talk last week and I should have realised that all was not right. Takashi, she was thinking of you even in her final days. She told me last Saturday that if anything ever happened to her, she wanted to leave you her house and her savings – and I must tell you she's saved an enormous amount of money.'

'Why?' Takashi asked, not able to take all this in at once. 'I wasn't even very close to her. Shouldn't you inherit the money?'

'She explained to me that times were good when your mother and I bought the family home and now that the

Japanese economy is not as strong as it once was, she's afraid you won't be able to manage as well as we did. She said that she wanted you and your future wife to have a comfortable life, just as I enjoyed when I was growing up, and so she wanted to leave you everything. You're never going to have to worry about money again, Takashi.'

'Unbelievable!' was the only reply Takashi could manage.

'I have to go now, we need to organise the funeral arrangements ... will you come out to Yokosuka?'

'Of course,' Takashi replied.

Takashi couldn't pick himself up off the floor for several minutes. He felt lost and very sad. Even though his grandmother had always been strict and stern with him, there'd been a few moments when he was a lot younger when she'd extended her kindness, and now that she'd passed away and left everything to him, her generous heart would never be forgotten.

Fifty minutes later, Takashi began walking towards the station, still thinking about his grandmother. He noticed small reminders outside that shadowed the fear that he'd felt the night before during the earthquake. Broken branches were scattered here and there. On the sidewalk, some sets of bicycles, lined three deep, had fallen to the ground. Various people scurried in and out of side streets, buying their necessities and then hurrying back to their homes. The damage was minimal but still worrying. *Had other parts of the country been so lucky? I should've finished watching the news*, Takashi thought to himself.

It was Saturday at ten a.m. and despite the earthquake and the shocking news about his grandmother's death, Takashi thought the best thing for him to do was to keep to his plans and spend some time with Masaya in Shibuya. The next few weeks ahead were going to be very sombre indeed as he and his family dealt with the funeral arrangements for his grandmother. Masaya was working minimal hours during the New Year break and Momo-chan had planned to go away with him to

Karuizawa in the Nagano Prefecture. They were leaving on Sunday morning, so Masaya and Takashi had decided to meet up on Saturday instead for their weekly shopping adventures. He felt brave and adventurous setting out to meet his friend after what he'd experienced the night before.

Takashi had just passed the MOS Burger outlet when his phone buzzed in his pocket. He saw Masaya's phone number flash up on the screen and, thinking that he'd decided to forego their plans to meet up, he answered with an annoyed and chastising tone. Takashi thought that his friend was probably still feeling a bit spent too from a lack of proper sleep and all the bad news.

'Have you decided to stay at home, Masaya?' he asked his friend. Masaya sounded distant and removed. This made Takashi stop dead in his tracks. He knew that Masaya had a strong personality. Surely nothing terrible had happened to him, he thought to himself.

'I can't believe it, Takashi,' Masaya cried. 'I just saw him last week and he looked so fit and healthy.' His voice was faltering. 'Not Kenji! Why did this have to happen to Kenji?'

'Slow down, Masaya,' Takashi told him. 'What happened? What's happened to Kenji?'

There was a pause. He heard Masaya's girlfriend Momo-chan's voice in the background. Something must have been really wrong if he was still at home when Takashi thought he'd been on his way to Shibuya.

'We can't go to Shibuya today, Takashi. You have to meet me in Yokohama. Kenji's in hospital! He's had an accident on his new motorbike. It happened yesterday during the earthquake. He's really hurt himself, but I don't know how bad it is. Please just meet me at Yokohama City Hospital.'

Takashi couldn't believe it himself. Not Kenji. Nothing like this ever happened to Kenji. He pulled himself together. 'I'm on my way. Don't worry, Masaya. I'll get a taxi to Shin-Kawasaki station and take the train from there. I'll be with you soon. I'll call you when I get to Yokohama station. Pick me up there,' he told him.

Takashi couldn't believe it, first his grandmother and now one of his best friends. He decided he'd go to Yokohama City Hospital and afterwards, he'd continue on out to see his parents in Yokosuka.

Reaching Shin-Kawasaki station, Takashi made a beeline for the platform. The mark of fear was set on the foreheads of each stranger around him because of the earthquakes. He kept telling himself that Kenji was going to be fine. He would be there for him and he knew that Kenji also had a close family. Over and over again, he repeated in his mind that Kenji would be all right.

The train ride to Yokohama seemed to take forever. On the way, a group of four children and their mothers climbed into Takashi's carriage. He guessed that the kids were all aged between five and seven. They were chatting away incessantly about the musical clock that they were going to visit outside the SOGO department store in Yokohama. It brought back memories for Takashi of when he was about five years old and his own mother had brought him and his brother to Yokohama for some shopping and to see this same mechanical clock that played a musical pantomime on the hour. They, too, had laughed and clapped at this small amusement. It occurred to him now that nothing that innocent could move him to that extent anymore.

An hour and a half later, Masaya and Takashi walked through the doors of the hospital, striding forward with obvious urgency. They needed to see their friend.

They asked for directions and arrived outside Kenji's room. Takashi looked at Masaya's frazzled face and he saw a fear in his eyes that he'd never seen before.

Takashi pushed the door open. The curtains were partly drawn and the light was dim. There was a strong stench of anaesthetic. Kenji's father was sitting by his son's side. He lifted a heavy head. His face was grey and his eyes spoke of sorrow. Takashi thought then and there that Kenji had really been seriously hurt and may be on his deathbed.

Kenji's father signalled to them to sit on the other side of the bed. Takashi looked at Kenji's face. It was bruised and battered. Masaya nodded at Kenji's right leg and Takashi saw it move a little. He let out a huge sigh of relief. Kenji was sleeping. Takashi went over to sit down next to Masaya and the three of them sat next to Kenji in silence for at least fifteen minutes before a doctor entered the room and checked the drip running from Kenji's right arm. A few minutes later, the doctor went to leave and Takashi followed him to the door. Outside the room, Takashi pressed him for information.

'Your friend has three broken ribs,' the doctor said. 'He's also broken his left leg in two places. Many of the scars on his face will heal, but his cuts are very deep and it will take some time.'

'So he's going to be okay?' Takashi asked with obvious relief.

'He certainly will, but he's a very lucky young man to be alive. We're still worried about his left leg. He may not be able to walk on it again for some time.' The doctor gave Takashi a short bow, turned abruptly and walked away quickly, as if he had no more time for questions.

Takashi returned to the room and nodded at Masaya. 'He's going to be okay, but his left leg is badly damaged,' he said.

Kenji's father looked at them. 'I can't believe this has happened. Look at my son. Why did I ever let him buy that motorbike? If only I'd known. Why? Why?'

It was soon time for Masaya and Takashi to leave. They paid their respects to Kenji's father and left. At the hospital exit, they saw a girl walking from the car park who looked a lot like Yuriko.

'Hey Masaya, does that look like Yuriko to you?'

'It couldn't be. How would Yuriko know anything about Kenji's accident? Anyway, that girl's got a fuller figure than Yuriko,' said Masaya.

'I saw her in Omotesando,' said Takashi. 'She's put on a bit of weight, but I don't think it's her.' Takashi stopped walking and crouched down with his hands over his eyes.

'What's the matter? Are you all right?' Masaya asked Takashi.

'I know it's an awful shock knowing Kenji's had this terrible accident, but I heard some even worse news this morning. My grandmother passed away yesterday.'

'I'm so sorry to hear that,' Masaya said to him.

'Thanks Masaya. Let's go,' Takashi said. He didn't feel it was appropriate to mention the inheritance. 'I need to get to my parents' house in Yokosuka.'

They headed to the station and went their separate ways. Takashi was well and truly exhausted.

—〰—

When Takashi reached the family home in Yokosuka, his mother had prepared him a delicious meal of croquettes, salad and rice and miso soup. After eating, he shared a few words with his father before taking a bath. Takashi really enjoyed the relaxing Japanese ofuro bath at his parents' house, as he only had a shower in his apartment. He sat down with his knees against his chest for a full half hour, allowing the hot water to envelop his whole body and the steam to waft over his head, after this, he prepared for bed. His mother had freshened up his room for him and he went to sleep early.

Takashi and his mother and father shared few words over the next twenty-four hours. Another death in the family had left a solemn mark on their house once again.

His father had contacted the Buddhist priest from the family temple and the undertakers. It was decided that Takashi's father would be the chief mourner for the funeral in two days' time.

Takashi stayed with his family for the wake and the funeral. He and his father wore conservative black suits on the day of the funeral. Many friends and family related to Takashi's grandmother attended to offer their condolences and offer a contribution. After the cremation, his grandmother's remains were placed in a kotsutsubo jar and rites would be held at her altar every seventh day until the forty-ninth day. Finally, his grandmother's ashes would be laid to rest at the family plot.

Takashi stayed with his family for a few days in Yokosuka to attend the funeral services before returning to his apartment in Kawasaki. He felt like he'd aged three years in the last few days, and the numerous small earthquakes that rocked the ground every now and again made him even more nervous. He hated those aftershocks that never gave anyone peace of mind.

That evening, as Takashi returned to his apartment, it was just starting to get dark. There was no wind, and not one leaf stirred in the bushes surrounding his building. He climbed the stairs slowly and with much effort; jiggling his keys to create a noise in the strange silence that surrounded him, before placing the largest of them in the lock of his front door. Takashi stepped inside and was just about to take off his shoes when another, much stronger, earthquake gripped him and he froze. The room in front of him started to sway, rocking back and forth as it had the other night. This evening however, it seemed even more severe.

Takashi pulled his door open again and immediately heard screams from his surrounding neighbours. Several people ran past him, heading for the stairs. Their faces were white with fear, and a couple of them yelled at Takashi to get out. Takashi tried to step out onto the landing that moved like an ocean. He grabbed the railing, but he was unable to move at all. Thirty seconds later, he felt confident enough to make it to the stairs. Gripping the rail as he moved forwards, he could see a group of people gathering at the bottom of the staircase. Water began to seep out through the cracks in the concrete path, causing liquefaction below their feet. The group collectively jumped onto the road as the ground moved even more violently.

Takashi waited at the edge of the landing, frozen against the railing, waiting for a break in this sea of movement. Two minutes later, he thought he saw his chance. Alone at the top of the stairs, he looked down at the group squatting on the road. The sight of them in a wide open space encouraged him to join them. Takashi gingerly placed a foot on the first stair, but the railing began to shake again. He glanced at the others and saw that a couple of them were pointing at the roof above him. He heard the building's caretaker scream at him to be careful. Looking up, Takashi saw the bicycle stem that had been thrown up on the guttering several months beforehand shoot out. It struck him square between the eyes and he fell back onto the landing. A sharp pain, like a needle penetrating his forehead, caused him to cry out as he started to black out. He screamed out and his howl reverberated in his head, sounding like a distant echo projected from somebody else's mouth.

He tried to keep his eyes open, but he was fighting to stay conscious. His mouth was dry and the feeling of losing control disturbed him. He fought to regain some kind of normality and he tried again to see what was happening around him. To his surprise, he thought he could see Masaya and Kenji standing at the bottom of the stairs, calling out to him. He wondered why they were there, and tried to remember what he'd been doing before he fell, but it hurt too much to think about anything. Takashi wasn't quite sure if he was conscious or not. His friends looked real enough. He saw his own arm stretch out before him as he reached out to them but Masaya and Kenji faded back away from him, laughing at him as they disappeared. The image of his friends was replaced by a whirlpool of green, red and blue lights rotating in front of him, and Takashi gave into the heavy feeling of unconsciousness. He lay back and stopped struggling against the pain. After that, he could remember nothing.

CHAPTER 19

Kindness will creep where it cannot go

Haruka was putting on her shoes on Sunday afternoon at the front door of her house when her father walked past.

'We were lucky nothing happened to us during the earthquakes, don't you think, Haruka?' he said to her.

'You're right, Father. Have you seen the news? What did they say about it on the TV?'

'They said the first earthquake measured 6.2 on the Richter scale and the second one measured 6.5,' her father replied. 'I hope we don't have any more this winter. I'm too old to be worrying about earthquakes.'

'I might be younger than you but they scare me just as much,' said Haruka. 'I'm going next door – I'll see you later.'

'To see your friend Yuriko?' he asked her.

'Yes, I'll be back at about five to help mother prepare the dinner.'

'I'll let your mother know.'

'Thanks,' Haruka said to him. She hurried over to Yuriko's and walked up the long drive to the entrance of her house.

Mrs Makimoto opened the door.

'Are you here to see Yuriko?' she asked Haruka.

'Yes – is she at home?'

'Yes, Yuriko's in her room. She's just come back from the hospital.'

'From the hospital! Is she alright?' Haruka asked.

'Yuriko's fine. Her friend was in a car accident.'

Haruka followed Mrs Makimoto into the house. 'Who was in the accident, Mrs Makimoto?'

'Don't you know?'

'No,' Haruka replied.

Haruka turned to head upstairs to Yuriko's room.

'I'm sure Yuriko will explain,' Mrs Makimoto said to her.

'Of course. Thank you, Mrs Makimoto,' Haruka replied.

Haruka reached the top of the stairs and knocked lightly on Yuriko's bedroom door. 'Come in,' said Yuriko.

'Hi Yuriko.'

'Hi Haruka, did you have a nice time in Kyoto?'

'No, not at all. Mrs Kurokawa was horrible to us, and it turns out that Jun is engaged to someone else. Why didn't you tell me about this?'

'This is news to me, Haruka. You know I've tried to ask Jun several times about how he feels about you, and he always changes the subject,' said Yuriko. 'And I'm sorry my auntie was so rude. She either really likes someone or she's perfectly vile towards them. My father can't stand her, so he rarely goes to Kyoto.'

'Well, that's the end of my relationship with Jun,' Haruka said.

'And what about your job in Kyoto?' asked Yuriko.

'That's fallen through as well. The manager who was leaving to go to live in the US with her boyfriend has decided to stay in Kyoto, so the position is no longer available.'

'Well, that's probably best, because you may have run into Jun if you'd been living in Kyoto – and anyway, I never liked the thought of you leaving. I would have missed you too much,' said Yuriko.

'Thanks,' Haruka said. 'I would have missed, you too. Your mother told me that you've just come back from the hospital. Who's been in a car accident?'

'It wasn't a car accident. It was a motorcycle accident. Kenji fell off his new bike during the earthquake.'

Haruka sat down on the edge of the bed next to Yuriko. 'Takashi's friend Kenji?' she asked Yuriko.

'Yes,' she replied.

'Oh no, that's terrible. Is he going to be alright?' Haruka asked, looking directly at Yuriko. Haruka was concerned about Kenji but also bewildered to hear about what had happened when she was in Kyoto. Kenji had been in an accident and Yuriko was sitting next to her looking very different. Yuriko's hair that she'd previously worn long and lanky had now been cut into a short, sleek bob. Her makeup was no longer caked on, but applied carefully and lightly, revealing a much more even and natural skin tone, just as Haruka had taught her. Yuriko's eyes looked bright and larger without the heavy, dark eye shadow she used to wear. Even her figure seemed fuller and much less gaunt.

'I'm worried about him,' said Yuriko. 'He's broken a few ribs as well as his left leg, and he has a lot of cuts and bruises on his face. His motorcycle helmet spun off him when he fell. I feel so guilty, Haruka. Kenji was on his way to visit me when he had the accident.' Yuriko suddenly clasped her hand over her mouth, as if she was trying to take back the words that she'd just uttered.

'He was on his way to visit you? Why was he visiting you, Yuriko?' Haruka asked, looking at her friend sideways.

Yuriko took her hand away from her mouth. 'I didn't tell you before you went to Kyoto. Kenji and I didn't want anyone to know,' she started telling Haruka. 'We went out to dinner a couple of times after he drove me home from Masaya's tavern, but I didn't say anything because Kenji wasn't looking for a relationship and I didn't want anyone to misinterpret our friendship.'

'What about Akiko?' Haruka asked.

'Kenji told me he'd never really liked her that much in the first place, but she kept coming to his restaurant in Ginza and he'd felt obliged to meet up with her.'

'Do you want to date Kenji, Yuriko?' said Haruka, drilling her friend.

'Yes, more than anything,' Yuriko replied.

Haruka smiled at Yuriko. *How could I have been so oblivious to what had been happening to one of my best friends and Kenji?* Haruka thought to herself.

'I feel like I've known Kenji for years,' said Yuriko. 'He told me that he feels the same way about me. I'm going to go to the hospital every day to look after him until he's well again. He told me that I make him feel better when I visit him.'

'That's wonderful, Yuriko. I'm so happy for you,' Haruka said.

Yuriko looked at her friend with concern. 'Have you spoken to Takashi?' she asked.

'No, he won't answer the phone. I really want to see him and tell him how much I care about him,' Haruka replied.

'What are you going to do, Haruka?'

'I could drive to his home in Kawasaki to see him, but I've never driven through Tokyo before, only around the Kanagawa Prefecture. I'm a bit scared of driving through those busy streets, especially after the tremors we've been experiencing.'

'I need to confess something to you,' Yuriko said. 'When I saw Takashi in Omotesando, I told him that you were planning a wedding with Jun in Kyoto, and he said that he'd given up on you.'

'Oh no,' Haruka groaned.

Yuriko placed a comforting hand on Haruka's shoulder. 'I think it's time you move on and find someone else. This relationship between you and Takashi is too messy and complicated,' she said.

It took a few minutes for Haruka to take this in. Her friend might be right, but this is not what she wanted to hear. Just the thought of not seeing Takashi again made her feel uncomfortable. Haruka rubbed her palms together and twisted her fingers. Her head felt like pins and needles, and her cheeks were burning up.

'Are you alright, Haruka?' Yuriko asked her.

'Not really ... I don't know what to do.'

'You need to take deep breaths.'

'I don't think I can forget about Takashi,' Haruka said to Yuriko, trying to breathe normally again.

'You'll be okay. Life has a funny way of working out. Look at me – I was so upset about Ryō, and then I met Kenji.'

Yuriko stood up and studied her image in the Bordeaux mirror on the facing wall whilst combing her hair through her fingers.

Haruka looked up at her. She was feeling a bit better. 'Your hair looks really pretty, Yuriko,' she said.

'Thanks. I had it cut last Friday morning.'

'And your skin looks better, too.'

'That's because I've stopped taking the weight loss pills. They were making me feel ill.'

'I told you they were no good,' said Haruka. 'Why don't you keep your hair like that from now on? It really suits you. Are you looking forward to starting your job at the interior design company next week?'

'I certainly am,' Yuriko replied.

Haruka stood up. 'Good to hear. I'm sorry, I have to go home now and help to prepare the dinner,' she said. 'Thanks again for meeting up with Takashi in Omotesando.'

'No problem, Haruka. I'm sorry it didn't work out with Jun. Well, you're right, it is just about dinner time and I wouldn't mind something to eat, as well. I'm famished. I think I'll make tempura for the family tonight.'

'Really?' Haruka replied. She was so pleased to see that Yuriko may have finally beaten her phobia about food. 'Would you like me to go with you to the hospital tomorrow after work?' Haruka asked.

'No,' she replied. 'Maybe next week.'

Haruka waved at Yuriko from the door of her room. 'Okay – tell Kenji that I'm thinking of him and that I wish him all the best.'

'Of course I will,' replied Yuriko.

CHAPTER 20

When things are at their worse they will mend

It took a while for Takashi to open his eyes. He felt dizzy, and he was trying to remember what had happened to him. He touched his forehead and felt a bandage. Leaning up on one elbow, Takashi slowly lifted his head and looked around him. He felt very strange, and yet everything seemed so normal. He saw that he was fully clothed and everything in his apartment was in order, just as he'd left it before he went to Yokosuka.

Light was coming through the window, but Takashi had no idea what time it was. He sat up straight, and in doing so, he noticed a note on the coffee table in front of him. The writing on the note pad looked like the scribbles of a child. Peering closer, Takashi saw that it was signed by the caretaker and that he'd written to say that he had Takashi's keys and he was checking on him every hour. Takashi thought this was odd, but he was too weary to worry about it. The hands on Takashi's watch showed 3:50 p.m. He thought that he must have slept for nearly twenty-four hours.

He was famished and decided to boil some water for a cup noodle. He was emptying the flavour sachet for his ready meal into the cup when the key turned in the lock of his front door. The caretaker popped his head through.

His smile was warm and parental, a side to him that Takashi had never seen before.

'You're up, finally,' the caretaker said.

'Yes, thank you,' Takashi replied. 'What happened? I can't remember.' He stopped preparing his meal and sat on the edge of his bed.

The caretaker removed his shoes and came over and sat on the floor in front of the television.

'I'm so sorry,' he said. 'You know that bicycle stem you asked me to remove from the guttering months ago, well....'

'Oh ... yes,' Takashi replied. He suddenly remembered being struck down by it on the stairs. 'Don't worry about it ... it was an accident,' he said to the caretaker.

No more apologies were necessary from then on. The caretaker explained how he'd called a doctor to Takashi's apartment after the earthquake and that he'd bandaged Takashi and informed the caretaker that he had a slight concussion, but that he was going to be absolutely fine.

The caretaker returned Takashi's keys and said that he'd check on him the following day before he scuttled back to his own apartment.

The weather would still be a little gloomy before the warmer breezes of spring began to infiltrate Takashi's flat. Three days after the second earthquake, Takashi was at home when his phone buzzed, and he smiled when he saw that it was his cousin Katsuro. He hadn't seen him since the funeral, and Takashi was eager to hear his news.

'Moshi moshi,' said Takashi. 'Is that you, Katsuro?'

'Yes, how's my favourite cousin?' he asked.

'Fine ... thank you for attending my grandmother's funeral.'

'That's okay,' he replied. 'How about those earthquake tremors – were you alright?'

'Fine,' Takashi lied, not wanting to cause unnecessary worry. 'What about you and Mika?'

'We're well, thanks,' he replied.

'How's work?' Takashi asked.

'Busy – and how's the study for your exams going?'

'I'm doing well in most subjects, except for English. My lecturer told me that I'd have to do a lot better in foreign languages if I wanted to work for a trading company,' said Takashi, lighting a cigarette.

'Don't worry. I don't speak English that well and there are many colleagues at my office that couldn't even get past a basic introduction when we were in Australia,' Katsuro reassured him.

'That's nice of you to say, Katsuro.'

'So you're okay? You don't sound bright at all, but I understand if you're not feeling your best.'

'As you know, my grandmother passed away but on top of this, one of my best friends, Kenji, had a motorcycle accident,' Takashi said.

'Oh no – how is he?'

'He's broken quite a few bones and he has lots of cuts and bruises.'

'That's terrible,' said Katsuro.

'Yes, but the doctor said that he'd be all right in a couple of months.'

'Well, that's reassuring,' Katsuro said with relief. 'And how's your girlfriend Haruka?'

'I don't think that I can call her my girlfriend anymore. She's interested in a rich guy from Kyoto. They may be getting married, and she's planning to move there for work.'

'Kyoto?'

'Yes, I'm trying not to think about it. I think she tried to call me a few times, but I didn't pick up. I suppose I'm afraid that she'll tell me that she doesn't want to meet up with me anymore.'

'Try not to worry too much. You can go out and meet someone else,' said Katsuro. 'You're young and you have a lot going for you, Takashi – and there are a lot of lovely girls out there.'

'I know, but this girl's different. Katsuro, it's so difficult to be positive at the moment with so many bad things happening. How do you do it, Katsuro? How do you remain so bright despite everything going on that seems to work against you?'

'I live by certain rules, Takashi. Maybe they're rules that can only help me, but they get me through each day.'

'Go on – explain them to me. They might help me, too,' Takashi implored.

'Well, let's see,' Katsuro began.

While Katsuro paused to think about his explanation, Takashi waited in anticipation. Although he knew it wasn't possible, he was hoping that maybe Katsuro could provide the secrets to a perfect life; a life filled only with happiness. He always seemed so happy to Takashi.

'I have this belief that a person has the ability to create and change the way their life pans out,' said Katsuro.

'Go on,' Takashi said.

'Um,' continued Katsuro, 'it's difficult to explain, but I kind of feel that when life gets difficult, it's important to keep the ball rolling forward … like in a soccer game. If you watch the Japanese soccer team, it's inspiring to see, because they'll never stop persevering until the final whistle. Despite any obstacles, they always try to push the ball forward towards their goal. And if you imagine life to be like a football game, then you can only try to persevere like the Japanese soccer team … right to the very end.'

'Yeees,' Takashi replied hesitantly, obviously not fully understanding.

'For example, if you stay in bed all morning, that ball – or your life – is not going to go anywhere, but if you get up and push yourself to do something, it could be anything, then the ball starts moving,' said Katsuro.

'I see. Yes, that makes sense,' Takashi replied eagerly. 'And we have the power to move that ball in any direction that we want. We just have to keep it rolling.'

'Exactly,' said Katsuro.

'Thanks. I'll try and remember that every morning,' Takashi said.

'That's the best time. Now I have some fantastic news to share with you,' said Katsuro.

Takashi could hear his grin beaming through the phone. 'Tell me,' Takashi said with anticipation. Now

Takashi was smiling again, because his cousin sounded so happy and so full of elation.

'Mika and I are expecting a baby!'

'Wow! Congratulations,' said Takashi. That was the best news he'd heard in a long time, and he was so happy for his cousin and his wife. Takashi was especially pleased for Mika, who'd been so depressed about not being able to conceive.

'When's the baby due?' Takashi asked.

'In July.'

'I bet Mika's happy.'

'Oh yes, she's thrilled.'

'Well, finally some good news. I have to come and see you both.'

'Whenever you wish, we love it when you come to visit,' said Katsuro.

'How about next weekend?'

'Next Saturday night it is. See you then,' said Katsuro.

Takashi put down his mobile, opened the curtains and allowed the sunlight to stream into the apartment. The ashtray was full of half-smoked cigarettes and ash. The room appeared to be broken up by many layers of thick smoke. He opened the door to the balcony and inhaled. The sweet fresh air danced its way into his nostrils. Takashi felt a little dizzy and slightly euphoric. He could see that a tablecloth of dust had settled on the top of the television, and he suddenly had a strong urge to clean.

It took him all afternoon to get his room and bathroom into order, and after he'd finished cleaning and put on a load of washing, he removed the bandage from his head and took a long shower; enjoying standing under the hot water for a full ten minutes before he washed his hair. Having rinsed off the shampoo, Takashi stepped out of the shower cubicle and dried off. With a thick white towel wrapped around his waist, he wiped the steam off the mirror, parted his hair and stood back to inspect himself. Takashi touched the bruise between his eyes and winced a little before making a funny face at his reflection. He was about to have a shave when he heard someone knocking on the door. He wasn't expecting anyone, but Takashi yelled at them to wait and threw on his jeans and a T-shirt.

He thought it was probably a door-to-door salesman, so Takashi slowly opened the door, planning to shut it again quickly if it was a stranger selling subscriptions. But when he opened it, he couldn't believe his eyes. Smiling sweetly in front of him, his dear Haruka was standing at the entrance.

Of course, Takashi was really happy to see her, but he was still not sure how she felt about him. He decided to play it cool. He pretended to be casual and slightly standoffish. He thought he probably just came across as awkward and uncomfortable.

'Come in,' Takashi said.

'What happened to you, Takashi? I've been so worried about you and you never answer your phone. Look – you have such a dark bruise on your forehead between your eyes – what happened?'

'I had an accident during the earthquake. It looks a lot worse than it feels. Don't worry about it; the doctor's seen it and he said I'd be fine … tea?' he asked her as she came in and sat down between the bed and the television.

'Yes please, green tea would be nice,' Haruka replied.

Takashi made the tea and they sat down opposite each other on each side of the coffee table. The repetitive whirring from the washing machine on the balcony acted like a calming musical score. He looked at her and wanted to be stern, but he ended up just looking a little silly. It was difficult to keep a serious face when all he wanted to do was smile and reach out to her.

Haruka took off her cashmere coat and grey woollen scarf. She looked very stylish in a cream polo neck sweater and tweed skirt. Wisps of hair were flying about her forehead, her brow was creased and her eyes looked strained.

'How did you get here?' Takashi asked her, helping her out of her coat.

'I came by train and walked from Kawasaki station.'

'Oh,' he replied. Takashi sat down, drummed his fingers on the table and pulled at his left earlobe. 'Were you all right during the earthquakes?' he asked her.

'Yes, but I was really worried about you, especially when I couldn't get through to you on the phone.'

'I'd almost given up on ever seeing you again because you were meeting up with Jun in Kyoto,' Takashi said, bracing himself. 'I need to talk to you about this. What I really want to know is if you're going out with Jun and whether you're planning to marry him.'

CHAPTER 21

The fortune of the house stands by its virtue

Haruka sat across from Takashi. Her head was lowered and her eyes were downcast. Her chin began to quiver and he saw a large tear slide slowly down her right cheek. It landed on top of the freshly cleaned coffee table, creating a tiny puddle. Takashi felt like his heart was ripping apart inside of him, but he didn't know what to say. He really didn't want Haruka to say anything and he regretted having asked her about Jun. He was afraid that she might say that this was the final time that she'd be able to meet up with him. Also, Takashi didn't want to hear about any special times that Haruka and Jun may have shared together in Kyoto.

'I'm sorry,' Haruka began to say. 'I'm sorry I went to Kyoto, especially when you were so stressed in the run up to your exams, but I thought I was doing myself a favour when I really wasn't, and my parents were so happy about me seeing Jun.'

'I thought they really liked him,' Takashi said to her. He couldn't face Haruka. He looked up at the top right hand corner of the room and he could feel a sting welling up in the back of his eyes. He held his head back and stiffened his shoulders.

'But when I found out the management position in Kyoto was no longer available....' Haruka said.

'Are you telling me that you're not moving to Kyoto?' Takashi asked, so pleased to hear that Haruka wasn't moving to the other side of the country.

'Yes. I'm definitely not moving to Kyoto,' she said. 'I know that I originally really wanted to live and work there, but not anymore.'

'Well, I'm glad all that's changed,' said Takashi.

They sat for a couple of minutes quietly taking this all in. Takashi wanted to give her the space to talk about everything.

'I need to tell you the truth, Takashi, because you've always been honest with me,' said Haruka after a while. 'Initially, I really wanted to visit Jun in Kyoto and my mother was just as keen for me to go there and meet up with his family. I can also tell you we were stupidly even expecting a marriage proposal, but as soon as we met his family again, we knew that we'd made a big mistake. His family was mean and horrible to me and my mother, and I felt that we were conned into believing something that just did not exist.'

'You know my mother has always been so keen for me to have everything that money could buy. It's been a lot more difficult for her since my father became ill, and even though he's recovered, I think my mother and I were trying to believe in a fairy tale.' Haruka paused for a moment and then looked straight into Takashi's eyes and continued, 'My mother and I were so impressed by his family's money and their connections with other wealthy people that we couldn't see how horrible they were.'

Takashi continued to look up at the top corner of the wall. His head was starting to feel a little bit like soft meringue. He continued to clench his shoulders.

'Honestly,' Haruka continued. 'When my mother met Jun's mother again, they didn't get along at all. As usual, his mother was haughty and condescending. I think she has much grander ideas for her son and Jun's just a thief and a liar.'

Takashi turned his eyes towards Haruka. They were moistening with joy. He felt his face turning red. He didn't know if he was embarrassed for doubting Haruka or just plain happy. He dared not utter a word just yet. He wanted her to finish talking. Takashi also wanted to feel more secure about whether she wanted to go out with him and him alone.

'So,' said Haruka, her eyes now sparkling, 'we returned to Tokyo after visiting various temples and gardens, and I realised how special you are. You have to believe me when I tell you that I've always thought that you're a wonderful person and now I know you're much nicer than Jun and I should never have gone out with him. I don't care if we have to struggle with money, because I love you and we'll make it work somehow.'

Takashi smiled at her and reached out to take her hand because he was so happy that she'd just told him she loved him. 'I love you, too, and what you've just said has made me very happy,' he told her.

'Good. Then we're okay?' she asked, squeezing his hand.

'We're okay,' he said as he drew her closer to him. 'We're better than okay and you don't have to worry, because I've just inherited a huge sum of money. The only sad part is that my grandmother, who left this fortune to me, has just passed away.'

'Oh no – I'm so sorry to hear that,' said Haruka.

Takashi adored her even more at that point for being more concerned about his grandmother than the inheritance.

'You know I'd love you with or without the money,' she said to him.

'Yes, I know that now,' Takashi replied. 'Haruka, did you hear what happened to Kenji?'

'I did. Yuriko told me.'

Takashi leaned back. 'How did Yuriko know?'

'Kenji was on his way to her house when he had the accident.'

'Why was he going to see Yuriko?'

'They had a few dates after he drove her home that night wc went to Masaya's tavern,' said Haruka.

'I see. So are they dating?' asked Takashi, quite startled.

'They went on a couple of dates, but Kenji made it clear to her that he didn't want a serious relationship, so they kept seeing each other as friends.'

'As friends!' Takashi exclaimed.

'Yes, she really likes him.'

'I see,' he said, still a little dumbfounded by this revelation.

'She's so upset about the accident, but she wants to be there for Kenji, and he's made her feel so much better about herself. She had her haircut recently and it looks really nice – and she's not as skinny anymore.'

'I know. I met her at the café. She's looking a lot better,' said Takashi.

'Takashi. Is Kenji going to be okay?'

'I'm not sure – we'll have to wait and see. We'll all look after him, won't we?'

'We sure will,' said Haruka.

'That's my girl,' Takashi replied.

He put his arm around her. 'Hey – I'd like to take you out to a nice restaurant this evening, Haruka,' he said to her.

She kissed Takashi lightly on the forehead, just above his bruise. 'No,' she replied. 'If you don't mind, I'd prefer to stay here with you. Let's get some snacks from the convenience store and have a feast here.'

Takashi hugged her tightly. Haruka really was a girl after his own heart.

EPILOGUE

Fortune waits on honest toil and earnest endeavour

The long, freezing winter ended, and the earthquakes were now a memory they all chose to forget. The spring brought Kenji back to good health. He was still walking with the help of a cane, but his doctor reassured him that he was making a speedy recovery and that he'd soon be able to get out and about without any assistance. Yuriko stayed by his side most days when she wasn't working at the interior design company in Shinagawa, and although Kenji and Yuriko insisted that they were just good friends, everyone suspected so much more.

Takashi did quite well in his final exams at university, but despite every effort, he was unable to take a position in a trading company due to his poor English. Instead, he began his first employment as an office worker at a bank – work he really enjoyed.

In April, the group came together for a few picnics under the cherry blossom trees. These seasonal flowers that come and go so quickly reminded them of the fleeting fragility of life and to appreciate what they had now, as it may well be lost again tomorrow.

Over the past six months, they had often gathered at Masaya's izakaya tavern to celebrate the end of each week. As well as this, Haruka, Momo-chan, Masaya and

Takashi met up to go out every Sunday and explore the shops in Shibuya and Daikanyama. They had lots more adventures, going out as a foursome.

In July, Takashi's family were thrilled to hear Katsuro's announcement that Mika had given birth to a baby boy, whom they named Naoki. Both mother and child were fine after the birth and in good health. Katsuro, Mika and the boy left Tokyo, earlier than expected, at the end of the summer to go and live in London, where Katsuro would work for a further four years.

Takashi enjoyed the rainy summer season that year, getting together with Haruka at his apartment and meeting at their favourite café on Thursdays. When the autumn began and the heat subsided, Haruka and Takashi began meeting up every other day, and they grew so much closer.

Three months later, Takashi sold his grandmother's house and moved in with Haruka into a new home in Shirogane which they bought with his inheritance. They both wanted to live a bit further away from central Tokyo, but a real estate agent suggested they take a look at this lovely home and instead of deciding on houses closer to their parents, they fell in love with the place and chose to live in Shirogane. The house had an ornamental Japanese garden that Haruka had always wanted and inside was a mixture of Western and Japanese rooms.

Takashi and Haruka had a new kitchen installed with smooth white granite worktops and a bathroom with all the latest mod cons. Adjacent to the house, their undercover double garage sheltered Haruka's Nissan March and Takashi's new BMW. The house was far too big for the two of them and they had plenty of room for Takashi's parents. They had spoken to them about this and decided that they would come and live in Shirogane with Takashi and Haruka when Takashi's father retired. Takashi always wanted to look after them in their old age.

Haruka told Takashi that her parents were struggling financially and although they were against it at first, Takashi eventually convinced them to accept his help.

Haruka's parents were so pleased that they didn't have to sell their house. Takashi also paid for his parents to spend a week with Haruka and himself in Hokkaido, where his mother could spend some time with her brothers and sisters. Even Katsuro, Mika and their boy Naoki flew over from London for the reunion.

Not long after, Takashi asked Haruka to marry him and she accepted his proposal. He just couldn't imagine his future without her. Takashi's mother suggested they go to Kyoto for their honeymoon, but Haruka and Takashi talked it over and they decided to go to Paris instead!

THE END

The research for this book was facilitated by:

Café hors et dans in Omotesando
Enya Izakaya in Shimokitazawa
Mrs Ayako Naritomi
Mr Katsunori Ariyoshi
Mrs Kurihara at Umi Gohan restaurant in Ginza
The Hotel Okura in Kyoto

. . .

Go to www.renaelucashall.com
to check out the free author's
Guide to Tokyo and Beyond.

Look out for TOKYO DREAMS
the sequel to TOKYO HEARTS

Lightning Source UK Ltd.
Milton Keynes UK
UKOW02f1902240415

250321UK00001B/7/P

9 781781 487693